DEAD

OF

WINTER

Dead of Winter

Kealan Patrick Burke

Print Edition

Visit the author at www.kealanpatrickburke.com

contents

DEAD
OF
WINTER

Kealan Patrick Burke

INTRODUCTION

A FEW YEARS AGO, while engineering our annual Christmas drink-a-thon, a friend of mine emailed me a picture he had drawn when he was a kid. At first glance it looked just like any other kid's drawing: crude, charming, and colorful, a depiction in crayon of good 'ol Jolly Saint Nick, cruising across the sky in a sleigh laden with gifts, while eager stick-figure children waited in the streets below, arms held aloft in typical childish glee.

At least, on first blush, this is what I *thought* I was seeing. But then I looked, *really* looked at the picture, and noticed something odd: Santa was flying upside-down, the gifts tumbling free from his sleigh to be smashed into dust in the (and this was something else it took a moment for me to notice) oddly *empty* streets.

I was immediately inspired to write a story based on that picture, and so, that's what I did. I dedicated the piece to my friend and emailed it to him. He responded with such enthusiasm, I decided that, in lieu of a Christmas card (which I'd been typically lazy in sending that year), I would send the story to everyone in my email address book instead. (This was back in the days when people emailed each other.) The response was positive, if a little glum, and this was to be expected. After all, Christmas is a time for sending happy, spirited, festive messages. The message I'd sent in "Doomsday Father Christmas" was anything but, and that went on to become a trademark characteristic of my annual "gifts". (One of my favorite writers, the reclusive Terry Lamsley, came up with the title for that story. Prior to his suggestion, it was called something lame, like "The Last Christmas" or some other Hallmark-channel sounding nonsense.)

The next year I sent out "Black Static", another sad and tragic piece. The year after that, those unfortunate enough to have shared their email address with me at some point over the past ten years found the depressing-as-hell short story "Visitation Rights", waiting in their inboxes. (When I read that story aloud to an audience at Noir at the Bar here in Columbus some years later, the crowd looked as if I'd just thrown up everywhere.)

But then, I do write horror stories, ladies and gentlemen. The dark stuff. And I have to admit, it gives me a kind of perverse thrill to imagine you now, cuddled up in the warm glow of a blazing fire, the tree lights blinking and throwing maddened shadows up the wall. Perhaps it's snowing outside and there's a classic Christmas movie on the TV, and there you are all cozy on the couch, book in hand, reading these words with a sinking feeling that maybe, just maybe, herein there lies little in the way of Christmas cheer. And you'd be right. What follows is grim stuff, my friend, Christmas *fear*, if you prefer. And if it rattles you a bit, gives you a chill despite the fire, then I've done what I set out to do with these tales.

Now let's get to it, shall we?

Before you catch a cold.

Or the cold catches *you*...

- Kealan Patrick Burke
December 201

SNOWMEN

THE TWO MEN STANDING IN RYAN'S BACKYARD were like irises in the eyes of winter.

And they were looking right at him.

The boy stood in his bedroom, the cold licking his wrists and ankles. He shuddered. His bed stood only a few tantalizing feet away. The window was even closer.

But he couldn't move. Not yet.

It was as if those faceless men playing statues in his back yard wouldn't let him look away. Wouldn't let him call his parents.

Not that that would do any good anyway. Dad had come home drunk enough to fill the entire house with the smell of sweat and whiskey. Mom was asleep on the couch, exhausted after carrying his father up the stairs and roaring abuse at him. They wouldn't be in any mood to entertain Ryan now. *Just your imagination*, they'd say.

But it wasn't his imagination. Nor a dream. He had blinked his eyes once, twice, three times. He'd pinched his arm hard enough to force him into stifling a yelp and there would be an angry red welt there tomorrow. He'd gone to the bathroom to pee and splashed cold water on his face...and when he'd returned, they were still there.

Two of them. One large, one small.

Faces in shadow, staring at him. He knew they were staring at him, could feel their eyes on him.

It was snowing again now but that didn't seem to bother them. They simply stood, unmoving, watching him with fierce interest. Waiting for something maybe. But what?

Again, he thought of rousing his parents. So what if they didn't believe him or got angry? At least he wouldn't be alone. At least then he could drag them in here and let them see for themselves that he wasn't lying or imagining things.

But would the men still be there?

Courage bloomed in him like a warm flower and he willed his legs to move.

In a heartbeat he was padding across the cold floor. He yanked the door open and the narrow hallway beyond yawned into view. His father was closest, so he hurried down the hall to his parent's bedroom and tapped once on the door, then entered the room, and—

—and stalled on the threshold, halted by memory. His eyes searched the dark, finally straining the shape of a bed from the meager light spilling in from the hall. A pale oblong held the crumpled shape of a wild-haired shadow, open-mouthed. Gasping and gurgling. Gasping and gurgling.

Can't wake him, Ryan thought, fearful. On his cheek, the latent print of an old wound rose like a submarine from the deep and brought a flush to his skin. The sound it brought echoing inside his skull was a mere whisper but the remembered threat was enough.

Wake me again you little bastard and I'll break y—

No. Suddenly afraid his presence would be enough to rouse the sleeping man, Ryan eased back, wincing in time with the creak and groan of the floorboards. He paused once more on the threshold, listening.

The shape on the bed shuddered, fell silent. Ryan's heart stopped.

He waited, hair prickling, for a sleep-muddled grumble. *"Whhhat're you doing in here, punkkk?"*

But it did not come. Waiting until the awful gasping and gurgling resumed, Ryan moved out into the hall, a heavy sigh momentarily drowning out the machinery of drunken slumber. He slowly turned the knob as far as it would go so the door would shut without a sound and was relieved when it did so without betraying him.

Safe. He was annoyed at himself for even thinking his father could help him. Dad was a mean drunk. Worse when roused from sleeping it off. And yet Ryan had intended on doing that very thing.

Dumb jerk.

There was not a doubt in his mind that his father loved him (even if he never said as much) and would never intentionally lay a hand on his son. But when he was drunk, he changed. Became possessed. He was a monster, who forgot the people who loved him, and lashed out at them as strangers. He hurt them, then wept in the morning when he saw what he'd done. A broken finger, a bleeding nose...a cut cheek.

A broken heart.

Ryan's breath whistled through his nose as he approached his bedroom. The door was opposite the stairs and now indecision cut through him. Wouldn't it be wise to check and make sure the men were still there before trying to wake his mother?

Sure it would. But what if they *weren't* there? It might mean they'd left, their staring game spoiled now that he'd moved away from the window, or it might mean they'd moved, looking for a way into the house to get him. The thought chilled him. But not nearly as much as the one that followed it: *What if they're* already *inside?*

Ryan swallowed, braced a hand against the wallpaper to steady himself. He listened to the sounds of the house. *Creak, groan, sigh, creak*, all in time with the soughing of the wind through the eaves. But weren't those creaks like footsteps mounting the stairs? Wasn't that groan like a stubborn door being carefully shut? The sigh the inexorable breath released at last by someone who'd been holding it?

Ryan began to tremble.

Creak, groan, creak...

Someone on the stairs.

Creak, creak, sigh...

"Hello?" Ryan's voice was tiny and quickly swallowed by the shadows hanging in the corners of the hall.

Creak. Creak. CREAK.

"Who's there?"

The wind answered him. "*Ryyyyaaaannnn,*" he was sure it said.

The footsteps drew closer.

This was not imagination either. Ryan felt his bladder let go, soaking his pajama bottoms as tears welled in his eyes. Not imagination at all and that was unfortunate, for at that moment, the lights flickered, just as the maker of those creaking sounds reached the top of the stairs and stepped onto the landing.

And there was no one there.

Lights buzzed. Shadows leapt, but the hallway was empty.

And from his father's bedroom, the suddenly reassuring sound of a hacking cough quickly became a gurgling snore once more.

Shivering, Ryan looked down at the puddle between his feet. He would have to clean it up before he got in trouble, but that could wait. He was already in trouble, but this kind of trouble was the very worst kind. The kind of trouble where you're not sure who's after you or why. All you know is that they are.

He stepped around the puddle, hand still splayed against the wall, the floor creaking and cold, the wallpaper he'd always hated whispering beneath his fingers, and swung into his room. The moonlight was splashed across his bed, smothering darkness in the folds where he had thrown back the covers when something had woken him up and drawn him to the window.

As it drew him to the window now, his body tensed, eyes wide and still moist.

They won't be there, he knew. *They won't be there because they're in the house with me, probably creeping up the stairs right now.* His certainty was reinforced by years spent watching horror movies at his best friend Larry's house on Halloween. Horror movies he knew his parents didn't approve of. Larry's parents didn't care. Sometimes they even joined them in watching them. In horror movies, the Thing That Was After You always stood motionless when you caught sight of it. Then, when you brought your parents back, babbling and screaming about the monster in your closet/on the ceiling/under your bed/outside your window and pointed at where you'd seen it, it would be gone. Making you a victim of something almost as bad as the monster: enraged parents. It would wait, then, until Mom and Dad were sound asleep before creeping out to kill you.

Now, he slowly stepped up to the window, his breath held, the feel of the wet pajama pants unpleasant against his skin.

They won't be there.

But they were, and in the same positions as before.

A sudden need to throw open the window and shriek *what do you want why are you standing in my yard?* down at them struck Ryan hard in the chest and he almost acted on it, until reason kicked back in and he stopped himself. That would be crazy. Opening the window might be just the move they were waiting for. His breath fogged against the glass and warmed his face.

He noticed something then, something awful, something he should have noticed before.

The air around the figures was still, unbroken.

They have no breath.

A noise in the hall made him jump. Creak.

Creak. Thump.

Ryan started to turn.

And one of the men in the yard moved.

Ryan gasped.

The move had been slight. So slight he almost hadn't caught it. The one on the right had tilted its head at him, as if confused by his actions, or the lack of them.

But as much as it seemed he had to, he couldn't dwell on that now, because this time, there was *definitely* someone out in the hall. The creaking of the floorboards he could have explained away as the same phantom walker he'd imagined on the stairs, but the thump could be nothing but a footfall.

Thump. There it was again.

Heart hammering madly, Ryan cast a quick glance over his shoulder, almost expecting to see the people in the yard had flown up and were leering in at him, their dead faces pressed against the glass. But no, they were still down there, watching. Ringed by leafless walnut trees.

Ryan padded slowly across the room and stopped a few feet from the door.

Somewhere out in the hall, a door opened. No attempt had been ma[...] to hide the sound of the knob rattling or the hinges creaking. Unstea[...] footsteps thumped one-two-three across the hall. Stopped.

Ryan's breath rasped. He shook. Folded his arms to steady himself.

Silence.

The fear within him seemed caught on the scale dead center betwe[...] relief and outright screaming terror. The footsteps were too confident, t[...] uncaring to be those of an intruder.

Dad?

Thump, thump, thump.

Again, they stopped.

The only bathroom in the house was downstairs. Ryan seized on t[...] memory of many nights waking to the sound of his drunken fath[...] struggling to negotiate the hallway, blinded by the light. His old man h[...] even fallen down the stairs once and sprained his ankle, though t[...] following day he'd claimed he'd twisted it while playing baseball with [...] cronies. But Ryan knew different. He'd heard it all, the rattling calami[...] the startled cry, the hiss of pained breath through clenched teeth, the c[...] for Mom.

The footsteps started again, and he almost cried out his father's nam[...]

But isn't that what they want you to think? a voice inside him caution[...] and he clamped his mouth shut. *That it's your father? You've seen two of the[...] down there, but who says there isn't a third?*

That was true. What if that was another one of them out ther[...] pretending to be his father? Trying to coax him out by fooling him in[...] feeling safe?

But the footsteps...they'd come from up the hall, from the direction [...] his parents' room and not the stairs.

You were asleep. One of them might have crept into your father's room.

He hadn't thought of that.

Call for Mom.

Yes. That was it. That was the thing to do.

But wait. What if that *was* one of them out there? Wouldn't calli[...] Mom lure her right into its arms?

His thoughts felt tangled, confusion overwhelming him until he found himself crying again. Soundlessly.

Why is this happening?

Thump, thump, thump, thump, THUMP! The footsteps jerked him out of his self-pity. He wiped the tears away with his sleeve and focused on the door.

Something grazed the hallway wall. *It's close.*

The thumping stopped.

Ryan's gaze fell to the light beneath the door. Twin shadows in the amber light, cast by the feet of whoever was standing outside.

"Dad?" he whispered.

Quiet, but for the wind hushing the night.

"Daddy?" he repeated and almost screamed, almost died of fright when an answer came.

"Ryyannn?"

The boy stepped forward, then back, his arm outstretched, uncertainty making a dance out of his movements.

It's a trick! They're trying to trick you!

But how could he be sure?

Don't open that door! They'll get you!

But what if it was his father, squinting at the door wondering what the hell was going on? Wondering if he'd imagined hearing his son's voice. Then he'd leave, go downstairs or back to bed. Leaving Ryan alone again.

And that couldn't happen.

"Ryyyaannn? That youuuu?"

The boy was at the door before he could change his mind.

IT'S A TRAP! DON'T DO IT!

Sobbing now, ignoring the protests of that fear-stricken inner voice, Ryan tugged the door open. The light blazed in his eyes, momentarily making a hunched shadow of the thing standing there. A noxious odor rolled across the threshold.

The voice inside him fell silent.

The house fell silent.

Then a board creaked as the shadow moved forward a step. "Ryan? What the hell's goin' on? Why you up?"

The tears came in a torrent Ryan was helpless to stop as he rushed forward and wrapped his arms around his father's waist, almost sending them both sprawling.

"Ryan? Hey! What's...?" Large muscular arms pried him loose and his father squinted down at him through eyes so full of red veins Ryan was amazed he could see through them. "What the hell's the matter with you? Why are you crying?"

"The win—" Ryan started to say, then wiped his eyes and rushed back into the bedroom. No. Had to check. The very worst thing that could happen now would be for him to tell Dad everything only to have the creatures in the yard vanish like they were supposed to. Like they did in the movies.

"Ryan?"

Everything was all right, Ryan realized, a surge of confidence brewing in his chest. Daddy was here now and even monsters with no breath would think twice before crossing his father. With the foul stink from the man clinging to him, a smell he now found infinitely comforting, Ryan closed his eyes and leaned forward to look out the window.

Please be there. Please be there. Please.

"Ryan? What are you doing?"

Ryan opened his eyes. And grinned triumphantly.

Relief swelled over him. "There's someone in the yard. Come look. They've been watching me all night. Two of them. They're not supposed to be there, are they Daddy? And they're not breathing!"

A weary sigh from behind him, followed by a click as his father switched on the light, casting a yellow oblong out onto the thick white snow beneath his window.

"There they are. Come look!" Ryan said, narrowing his eyes, unable to stem the excitement now that his lonely night of terror was over. Whatever those things down there had come for, they wouldn't get it now.

He rubbed his fists over his eyes. Felt the grit of forgotten sleep come away.

He looked down and pointed at the two figures, now bathed in hazy light.

And froze.

Even from here he could see the mistake he'd made in the beginning thinking there were two men down there. There weren't. Nor were they the wicked monsters of his imaginings.

One of them was a woman. The one with the tilted head

(*because it's coming off*)

was a woman.

His mother. Glittering in the light, ice forming a skin over her body, holding her in place, holding her still and firmly planted in the mound of snow at her feet.

"Ryan? What are you doing?"

Ryan began to tremble, a whine building in his throat, trapped there with all hope of a scream.

Daddy sounded as if he needed to clear his throat. Daddy's reflection grew bigger in the window. Beneath which, another version of Daddy, the *real* Daddy, stood in his very own mound of snow, arms pinned to his sides, skin alive with crystals, mouth open and filled with snow.

Staring up at him.

The shadow filled the window, draping darkness over the figures frozen below.

Ryan watched it, allowed his eyes to meet the reflection of the liquid blue sparks hovering just above his head.

Gasping and gurgling, a sound he had mistaken for his father's snoring. He now realized it had been nothing so innocent. As icicles met his skin and darkness filled his eyes, all awareness of pain and death swept away from him, leaving him with one single shred of a thought.

That in the morning there would be three snowmen in the garden.

DOOMSDAY FATHER CHRISTMAS

ON A HILL OVERLOOKING THE CITY, the old man sat quietly in his sleigh, the reins still gripped in his gloved hands. His hooded gaze roved over the houses down in the valley to his right, a mass of twinkling lights brimful of expectant children, each one led into sleep by the promise of what the morning would bring.

And what, the old man asked himself, *will the morning bring for me?* Immediately the answer presented itself, courtesy of his wife's disembodied voice, which he cherished and abhorred in equal measures, depending on the wisdom it proffered at any given time. *You get the satisfaction of bringing joy to so many children.*

"And how do I do that?" he asked aloud, his breath forming ghosts around his face. At the head of the reindeer, Rudolph, his muzzle badly scarred around the faintly luminous bulb of his nose, glanced back over his shoulder, as if he thought he had been addressed. The old man looked at him and felt a twinge of sadness. Of them all, of everyone on earth, this poor dumb animal was probably the closest he had to a friend. It had sacrificed much to stay by his side, enduring the bullying of its brethren, the life-draining effect of the genetic anomaly that made its nose seem to glow in sympathy with the moon, the callous hunters and their desperate plight to return home with his antlers for a prize.

"It's okay, boy," he told the animal, and it watched him for another moment, doubt in its watery eyes, before joining the others in grazing.

They need you, Nick, now more than ever, his wife said, and he frowned. More and more these days she spouted Hallmark sentiments designed to allay the doubt that grew worse each passing day. Once, she'd been right, but he suspected even she didn't believe her words anymore. They had seen and endured too much over the centuries, had witnessed too many changes for the worse. He didn't however, greet her remarks with hostility, at least not in her presence, for he feared what might happen if he disabused her of what little festive spirit still lingered within her. She might lose her smile, and with it, all remaining hope that things would ever again be like they used to be. There was already enough distance between them, committed as she was to supporting a pursuit he no longer believed in.

Prancer snuffled and shook his head, rattling his bridle. The old man chose to think of it as coincidence, and not agreement, or denial of his thoughts. He looked down at his hands, their deterioration visible through the rents in the material. The fingers were thin and spindly. For a long time, he had not aged, the clock stopping at sixty-one, but it seemed now that he was being punished for his cynicism and ennui. For his doubt. For daring to question whatever higher (or lower, he sometimes thought) power was responsible for this curse. Immortality was apparently a privilege that could be revoked if he failed to fully immerse himself in the role assigned him. And so every year, he did his job.

But he was tired now. So very tired.

And though the world continued to celebrate the seasons and the days marked for joy, he saw little joy on their faces. Instead he saw billboards and commercials instructing exhausted parents where and when to spend money they didn't have on extravagant toys that would be forgotten or broken in six months. He saw the transient delight on the children's faces, a facade that hid their disappointment at not receiving something bigger, better, and more expensive. He saw the parents, broke and on the verge of divorce, drinking too much to avoid confronting the reality of their situation, and each other, or arguing silently while their children grew bored and flipped idly though channels on the TV, hardly seeing anything at all. And on every channel, between commercials designed to inflame the greed of the child and make them rue their choice of gifts, were visual representations of the old man, ho-ho-ho'ing his way down chimneys far too small to accommodate him, or rescuing some wretched waif from heartbreak and loneliness, which only instilled in lonely children hope that would never bear fruit.

But who, he wondered, *will rescue me?*

Ultimately, he realized that he was, despite the centuries of dedication, little more than a commercial himself, an ancient billboard with an unchanging message. He represented expense, often exacerbating the pressure on people ill prepared to handle it. Inadvertently, he had sent more people to their deaths than he had saved. Like those commercials, he reminded parents of their obligations and children of their entitlements, then watched from afar as it all came apart. He never entered the houses, and this was a good thing, particularly in the current climate, for he would no doubt be arrested, or shot at. Contrary to the myth, he did not ride a sleigh laden with enough presents for every child in the world. He had no presents at all, for that was not his job. He rode a sleigh empty but for intangible promises.

In the old days, he had yearned to live up to the world's interpretation of him, even going so far as to sell most of the belongings from his mortal life, now classified as priceless antiques, so that he could afford to buy presents for at least a thousand children. Even then, even after his overjoyed wife fashioned a large red sack from old bed sheets, he was faced with the problem of distribution. Remarkable flying reindeer or no, there were still laws, and he could not just insinuate his way into people's houses. So he left them in the mailboxes of the impoverished, only to have a third of them destroyed or stolen. Another third had been lost after he failed to consider the impact the weight of so many presents would have on the sleigh, and the poor beasts tasked with pulling it. Consequently, on Christmas Eve in 1965, roughly three hundred packages rained down on the Sahara Desert, where they lay broken and useless until the sand erased them forever. Even the presents that made it to their intended recipients left him feeling curiously apathetic. He supposed it was because, unlike the iconic figure he'd inspired, he could not see the reactions of the children who received them, could not see their elation, or disappointment. He suspected despite their poverty, there were more of the latter than the former. After all, it would be sheer coincidence if any of the gifts he gave them were the things they had asked for.

Despite the enthusiasm that marked his departure from home that year, sleigh loaded with presents, it was the last time he attempted to fit the world's image of him. There were simply too many variables, too many obstacles, with no way of knowing at the end of it all if it had been worth it.

And unlike the jolly fat man in the red suit, he was an emaciated figure, drained of spirit. His suit was tattered and torn and more mottled maroon than red. His boots had holes in the soles, and his jolly red hat had long since blown away, exposing a bald head threaded by the scars earned in those first clumsy days when he'd had to learn quickly how to fly a vehicle designed to travel on the ground, pulled by intemperate animals who believed themselves above such menial labors.

Every year, he inspected his sleigh, promising he would give it a much-needed lick of paint, or repair the buckled running boards, knowing he would not. He would ease himself into the seat with its ineffective threadbare cushion, and let the reindeer take him on yet another tour of the nightworld. All the while thoughts of the children in those houses beneath the chipped and splintered wood of his sleigh plagued him. He could not help but picture the starving children down there, the dirt-smeared faces of the suffering, the young ones hiding behind the rubble as shells exploded mere feet away, the dying, the diseased, the kids locked in cellars by parents or perverts... It made him feel like a cold-hearted observer flying over hell.

This, he feared, was closer to the truth than he cared to admit.

And though his wife stridently objected to such theories, she was never able to convince him that it wasn't what she herself believed.

The horrible reality of it was this: He existed to turn the minds of children away from the true meaning of Christmas, away from God, by appealing to their greed. To appease the greed, the parents suffered. And yet no one ever thought of the old man as anything but benevolent. How shocked they would be if they knew he thought himself closer to an emissary of the devil.

He had flown through wars, concealed by smoke, dodging artillery not meant for him, coughing through muddy fields occupied by shifting specters of mustard gas and littered with bodies. He had watched cities burn and drown and crumble. He had watched and wept from afar as children were led to gas chambers. He had seen them murdered by the hundred at the hands of monsters.

And he, their alleged patron saint, had done nothing.

Disgusted, he whipped the reins, ignoring the caustic look from

Dasher as the reindeer ceased their feeding and tugged the sleigh along the hill, headed for the edge and the air beyond.

People had seen him, he knew. If there was one joy he could claim, it was that. Over the years there had been people on the street, young and old alike, who had glanced up and caught sight of him sailing through the air. The children had screamed and pointed and danced with delight. The adults had stared, stricken, unable to reconcile what they were seeing with the remembered devastation at the hands of their own parents, who had told them in earnest, that there was no such thing. And on such occasions, the old man had grinned and waved and yelled "Merrrrrry Christmaaaaas!" at the top of his lungs. It had excited him, however briefly, had restored for a while the jubilation he'd once felt knowing that, for some, it didn't matter that he wasn't the Santa Claus they grew up believing in, or had been *programmed* to believe in. For some, he simply represented hope, and dreams made real. Proof that there was sometimes more to life than the grind, the pressure, the struggle. Proof of magic.

It had been a long time since he'd been seen, but tonight, that would change.

As he angled the sleigh toward the moon, the reindeer huffing, he did not look down at the snowy streets sweeping beneath him. There was no need. These days children did not stay up late watching for him. They did not sneak out into the cold and stare up at the sky, hoping for a glimpse, for confirmation that what the other kids were telling them at school wasn't true. Nowadays, they stayed inside, eyes wide and glassy as they watched lies on their computer and television screens, where sincere-sounding reporters stood red-faced and shivering beside a graphic insert that showed a fictional Santa's flight-path in real time. No expense was spared on perpetuating the myth, while elsewhere other children died of exposure or starvation, or abuse, and still others crumbled as their parents gave them the truth they'd prayed was not there and therefore dealt a final, killing blow to the wonderful world of fantasy and magic. *Santa Claus is not real.*

To the old man currently riding upward into the night sky, the cold wind biting his sallow cheeks, the moon looming large before him, he hated that the truth those parents so callously shared was the ultimate and indisputable one. *He* was real. But Santa Claus was not, and never had been.

Tomorrow, the evidence of the lie would be laid out for all to see, and perhaps it would instigate a change for the better, an embracing of magic one last time. Perhaps it would do the opposite, forcing people who had once believed to become bitter and critical of anything they could not see for themselves. Perhaps it would turn them further away from God. Or, perhaps it would mean nothing at all.

Nick, don't, said his wife. *It doesn't have to be over.*

There was, as always, little conviction in her voice. She knew, as well as he did, that they had reached the end of whatever path they'd been instructed to follow. He had once read a line about every species being able to sense its own extinction. He thought there might be something to that.

"Everything has to end eventually," he said, the wind of his passage whipping the words from his mouth.

One final ride, he thought, cracking the reins. The reindeer, their hooves pounding nothing but the air, quickened the pace. Rudolph looked back, the light in his nose brightening the closer they got to the moon. There was a knowing sadness in his dark eyes. The old man nodded at him and smiled, an acknowledgement of their friendship, of their eternity spent together in service to some unknown force.

As the sleigh crested an invisible wave, the reindeer dipped its head and twisted sharply around, turning the sleigh upside down. The other reindeer, forced to follow its lead, kicked and protested, but it was too late.

The old man fell from the sleigh, smiling as he plummeted toward the earth. The wind snapped at his clothes, tore free his gloves. A boot slid off and was lost to the night. Someone would probably get rich from selling it on eBay. He grinned. Overhead, the reindeer carried on, led by a small blue star, their sleigh bells ringing like the chiming of a clock counting off the moments before the end. They were headed for the moon and whatever resting place would have them.

The lights of the city rushed up to meet the old man, an ugly sulfuric glow that made him think of the poisonous air ghosting its way across those European battlefields.

Time marches on, he thought, seconds before the impact. *And we are soon forgot.*

There were no faces in the windows, watching.

BLACK STATIC

W HAT DATE IS IT?" my father asked.
The television was off. On the screen I could see the reflection of his face, and the snow, as if the world outside our window had lost reception.

"The 25th," I reminded him, trying hard to keep the exasperation out of my voice. "Remember?" It wasn't his fault his mind was going, or that every second sentence emerged tethered to the end of a ropy cord of drool. *It'll require a great deal of patience*, the doctor had said, *And it'll exhaust you, but remember he can't control what's happening to him. Neither can you.*

"It's Christmas."

"Oh," he said.

I looked down at the milk and cookies I had prepared for him. Such a childish ritual, one I could scarcely reconcile as a memory from my own turbulent childhood. But here we were. Roles reversed. He'd lost his mind, I'd lost everything else.

"It's cold in here. I can see my breath. Why is it so cold?"

"I'll take care of it."

"Christmas," my father grumbled as I delivered his treat. Standing there facing him, I saw that he looked little different from his reflection in the television screen. Haggard, drawn, eyes sunken. Only the snow was gone, but all I had to do to see it again was raise my face to the window, to the dizzying maelstrom of white and the children dashing past the yard trailing gleeful screams as they pelted each other with hard orbs of snow and ice and pretended it hurt. "Christmas for whom?"

Beyond the haze of white, Christmas lights twinkled feebly like lost memories struggling to resurface.

"For me, Dad," I replied.

He shifted uncomfortably in his tattered armchair. Brought his face close to the glass and sniffed. "There's something in my milk."

The snow was mesmerizing. A temporary escape. A blanket beneath which forty years of contempt could be buried and forgotten. A shroud beneath which anything could be hidden.

I looked at him. At the look of desperate concentration on his face.

I looked at the milk.

Black specks. Black static. In a moment he would drink it because he would forget why he ever thought he shouldn't.

"This year it's just for me."

VISITATION RIGHTS

D ID YOU GUYS ALREADY HAVE DINNER?" I ask the two little girls in the rearview mirror. The green dashboard lights lend my face a ghoulish cast.

Isabelle continues to stare out the window at the late Christmas shoppers dashing through the snow. Her arms are folded. She's not done sulking.

Kara, a year younger than her sibling, so perhaps not yet mature enough to completely absorb the full potency of her mother's hatred of their father, joins her sister in watching the snowy streets and stores blazing with multicolored lights, but shakes her head.

"Well then I'm glad I put a turkey in the oven!" I tell them. It's a microwave meal, but they don't need to know that, though I'm sure the taste will give it away. "Everyone hungry?"

No response. Isabelle has tears in her eyes.

In the mirror, my smile looks desperate, and frail.

I return my gaze to the road. I shouldn't be driving in this. The snow makes the windshield look like a TV screen with bad reception. Half-glimpsed figures rush through the lights, heads bowed, as unaware of me as I am of them. My attention is focused on my daughters, who have brought the cold of this Christmas Eve into the car with them.

"You excited about your presents?"

Again, Isabelle says nothing. Kara only blinks.

Somehow, I manage to guide the car out of the shopping district without incident. The festive lights and their associated—if alien—cheer vanish, replaced by whirling dervishes of snow turned red by the brake lights as I turn into our—into my—neighborhood.

Here the houses are vague, dispirited, dark-eyed shapes hunkered against the cold. The wheels of the car slide a little in the slush, but I keep my small, battered Toyota from hitting the curb and offer the girls a reassuring smile neither of them sees.

Then my home, which looks no less unwelcoming than any of the others, and I kill the engine. Listen for a moment to the ticking of the snow against the windshield as it tries to erase the outside world. Listen for a moment to the hitching breath from Isabelle's mouth as she struggles not to cry. Listen to the sniffling as Kara bravely fights with a cold.

"All right girls...we're here!"

And I listen to the erratic thumping of my own heartbeat as I swallow and open the door.

* * *

"Makes yourselves at home. Go on. Take your coats and boots off," I tell the girls as I hang my coat on the rack by the front door.

They look inclined to do no such thing. They just stand there, looking small and miserable, and lost. Isabelle is still pouting, but as frustrating as it is, I know better than to chastise her for it. It's one of the many privileges I lost with custody, and one that would only exacerbate things now. Kara is shivering despite the cloying heat in the apartment. It's always warm in here, but today I set the thermostat higher knowing the kids would be coming back with me. I guess I didn't think getting them here would take as long as it did.

I stamp snow from my shoes and offer them reassuring smiles though it hurts my heart to see them standing close together as if seeking solace from some terrible threat. Nightly I relive the warm cherished memories of their faces lighting up at the sight of me coming home from work, especially on Christmas Eve, my arms laden with gifts I made a show of pretending were not for them. I remember the clean scent of them as they wrapped their arms around me, the softness of their lips against my cheek, the laughter, the joy.

The love.

"Right then," I say, rubbing my hands briskly together and moving past them to the kitchen. "Off with those coats or you'll be more roasted than the turkey. I'll get dinner on the table and we can eat. And after that, we can exchange gifts."

As I tug open the fridge, I wince. Using the word "exchange" was a force of habit. Of course they have no presents for me, nor should I have expected any. I promised them gifts last Christmas, and on their birthdays, and forgot on each occasion thanks to self-pity and a bottle with a man's name on the label. So I expected wariness and doubt. I expected awkwardness. I didn't, however, expect fear, distrust, and coldness.

"What I mean is," I tell them, yanking three microwave dinners from the fridge and nudging the door shut with my knee. "You guys can unwrap the gifts *I* got for *you*." The chill from the boxes feels like Heaven on my calloused fingers. I set the meals down beside the microwave and turn to look at the girls. "Come on in here! Sit down! I won't bite."

They don't move. They just keep staring at me, their eyes moist. I notice they've moved closer together though. Kara's hand has found its way into the crook of her sister's arm. Isabelle has her gloved hands shoved into her pockets. Both have their hoods still up.

I turn back to the meals. Maybe the smell of food will entice them to join me.

"Not quite as fancy as the dinners your Mom makes," I explain as I set the timer. "But I think you'll like it. The secret is lots of gravy." I chuckle to myself to keep from sobbing.

It's been over a year since I've seen my children. A year is a long time to be misrepresented by an ex-wife who hates you. And she has every right to hate me. I was a drunk, and a violent one, and yes, I hurt her more than once. Sometimes, physically. Often, emotionally. But I never hurt our children. Never did anything but love them, and it angers me to see what she has done to them.

I turn back again to face my girls. Still standing there, still watching.

"Girls, I want you to come in here. I want you to come in here and sit down."

They don't.

I try to measure my tone, but it's getting more difficult. They're looking at me like I'm some kind of a monster. Maybe I was, once, but never to them. Never. She has no right to make them think of me that way, and they have no right to believe it.

"Isabelle...Kara...I'm not going to ask again. Please come in and sit down so I can talk to you. You're not being very nice to me right now, treating me like this."

Kara's lower lips trembles.

A tear spills down Isabelle's cheek.

I begin to tremble. "Isabelle...why are you crying? I haven't done anything to you, have I? I thought we were just going to spend a little time together for Christmas. I thought we were going to have a nice Christmas Eve dinner and—"

"I want Mommy," Kara whimpers, and now she is crying too.

"What?" I heard what she said, but I don't want to have heard it. It's a cold finger against my heart, a clenched fist in my throat. I don't want them to want their mother. Just once, just for a little while, I want them to want me.

Snow patters against the windows. The wind moans in the eaves. A symphony of loneliness that will never have a reason to change.

"Ok, ok," I say, and throw up my hands. Force a smile. "Gifts first, then dinner, and then I'll take you home, how does that sound?" I head into the living room, resisting the urge to grab my children as I pass them and throttle the sense their mother has contaminated back into them.

"We don't want gifts," Isabelle sobs. "We want to go back to Mommy."

At the wretched looking tree, which I surreptitiously salvaged from the reject pile at the back of Carson's Christmas Tree Lot, I feel my muscles tense and swallow to clear my throat. "You're being silly. Every kid loves gifts. Just wait until you see what I got y—"

"We want Mommy now. Bring us home," Isabelle says. "You weren't supposed to bring us here. You weren't supposed to take us away."

Bathed by the sulfuric glow of the cheap lights I have strung chaotically around the palsied limbs of the tree, I bite my lip and drop to my knees. There are only two presents there, but they represent three weeks' worth of overtime and worse, three months of sobriety.

"Just wait until you see..."

"We don't *want* your stupid presents," Isabelle yells, and stamps her foot on the floor, startling me. "We want to go home to Mommy, *now*."

I can't move. I'm on my knees with my hands poised over her present, and I can't move. I feel as if my insides have turned to solid ice, my brain to fire. The trembling worsens. God help me I want to slap my little girl across the face and tell her to never speak to me like that again. That if she understood what life in this shithole little apartment has been like without her, without Kara, without her mother and the affection with which they used to treat me, that she would forgive me my trespasses and rush into my arms. She would gladly accept the gift I bought her then. She would gladly accept me as part of her life again. She would care.

I weep, silently, as I unwrap the gift. I'm blocking it from her view, so she can't see what it is. But that hardly matters now, does it? It could be a pony, a car, a million dollars, and it wouldn't matter. She only wants her mother.

"It's a cell phone," I whisper, running a finger over the small rectangular box. "An expensive one. I bought it..." My throat closes, trapping a sob. I wait. Try again. "...I bought it and programmed my number into it so that, even if you didn't want to talk...you could send me a text now and then." The sobs come, wave after wave of them rippling through me as I push the gift aside and reach for Kara's. I can barely see it through the ugly orange and dazzling white kaleidoscope the tears have made of my eyes. Blinking furiously, I tear open the wrapping paper and roughly fling it aside.

"For you, Kara, honey." I raise the box to show it to her. I am heartened to hear her give the slightest gasp. "A Sassy Sarah doll. The clerk at the store told me they're the coolest thing out there right now." I continue to hold it up for a moment, waiting, wanting her to take it. When she doesn't, I let it fall to the floor and stand, my knees cracking painfully.

We are a tableau of pain and misery and fear.

I watch them, searching their small faces for the slightest hint of love.

And find none.

"Okay," I tell them. "Let's get you home. You can still take the gifts if you want them."

They don't, of course.

* * *

They say nothing on the ride back to their mother, even when I tell them I'm sorry for scaring them, even when I tell them the words I've rehearsed in my gloomy apartment every night for over a year. Even when I open the car door for them and tell them I hope we can try again some time.

They have nothing to say, and that says enough.

Lit by the car's headlights, our passage up the snowy cross-studded hill is a somber one.

"Happy Christmas," I whisper to Isabelle, as I lay her body back into her grave. The wind freezes my tears.

"Happy Christmas," I whisper to Kara, as I lay her down in the hole, which is not as deep as I dug it thanks to the endless snow.

I return to the car and retrieve the shovel, grimacing as the handle chafes against my calloused hands.

And as I fill my children's graves back in, my eyes stray to the headstone next to theirs, to my wife's grave, and I wonder if she will ever forgive me, if maybe that's where a wiser man would have started. If maybe, just maybe, some day she might give me another chance.

Hope is a dangerous thing, but without it, what else is there?

I allow myself a small smile.

We'll see.

Valentine's Day is not so far away.

HOME

MONDAY. CALLUM FINISHED WORK AT FIVE-THIRTY. By that time the polar vortex had already swept through town, half-burying everything in smooth mounds of wet white dust and driving everyone inside who didn't need to be out. Even the traffic was mercifully sparse, though apparently only the insane and the idiotic remained.

He slowed the Jetta to allow a lady driver to go ahead of him, something, for some reason, she seemed reluctant to do, her indecision prompting angry honks from the cars behind his own. He sighed. Punishment for his manners. He wondered why he'd bothered. Checked his watch. Slammed his hand down on his own horn and the woman waved and hurriedly guided her Honda into the opening he'd given her. Traffic moved forward an inch and the light turned red.

Callum cursed. Today was his daughter's birthday. Of all days to be late.

It began to snow again.

* * *

The trucks had plowed the streets around his neighborhood, but nobody had bothered to shovel his drive or sidewalk, which forced him to temporarily park on the curb until he had a chance to do it himself. Leaving the car out here for the night was inadvisable unless he wanted to wake in the morning to find it buried by the plows.

But the unbroken snow did tell him one thing: Nina and Barb weren't yet home, which meant his tardiness wouldn't register. Not only that, but they'd be grateful that he'd cleared the snow for them by the time they arrived. All in all, he'd end up their hero, a status he very much enjoyed, particularly given that Nina was sixteen today and seemed not to care about anything much anymore if it didn't involve trashy music, floppy haired boys, and reality TV.

He parked. Opening the car door was like pushing a shopping cart through mud. He stepped out into three feet of snow that both froze and soaked the legs of his slacks. Grimacing, he struggled through the opaque depths, his briefcase clutched to his chest as if he were a pioneer attempting to ferry an infant to safety. The drifts made his yard look like a scale model of the Himalayas. Around him, the street was deathly quiet, as if the snow had buried all sound other than his labored breathing and the crunch-squeak of his passage through it. It seemed to take an inordinate amount of time for him to reach the door, but here, thankfully the porch overhang had dissuaded the drifts, though the welcome message on the door mat was obscured beneath a skin of white.

Eyes watering, the hairs in his nostrils like steel wool, skin prickling with the cold, he retrieved the key from beneath the mat, having lost his own in the first severe snow a few days before, and opened the door.

Inside, he was greeted with an immediate and beautiful breath of warmth, and he thanked Barb for thinking to leave the heating on while she went about her errands. He could, after all, clearly remember a period in which such considerations would have been far beyond her, right around the time their marriage suffered a near-fatal polar vortex of its own.

Callum set his briefcase down and kicked off his shoes. His socks were saturated, so he slipped those off too and left them all in a heap by the door.

2

It took him almost an hour to shovel the driveway and the sidewalk, by which time he was drenched in sweat beneath his coveralls. His muscles burned. He was not one given to regular exercise, something he reminded himself for the hundredth time needed to be properly addressed and rectified. Entering through the man-door, he triggered the garage door, then got back in his car and parked it inside. He took a last look at the shoveled driveway, already paling beneath the still-falling snow, and the dirty knotted clumps flanking it, and let the garage door rumble closed.

From there, he let himself into the mudroom, his wet clothes already doing the rounds of the tumble dryer. Now, he paused their revolution and, after stripping out of his hat and coveralls, added them to the load.

After changing into jeans and a knit sweater, he stood in the mudroom, the machine whumping and humming behind him, and realized how quiet the house was, how quiet it had been since he'd come home. Where was everyone? It was Nina's birthday, and he felt a tiny worm of worry in his belly that he might have forgotten some plan, some celebration elsewhere they might have mentioned to him while he was distracted. Racking his brains turned up nothing, so he went to the kitchen, to the fridge door, which served as their reminder and announcement board.

A gust of wind buffeted the house, the snow hissing against the windows.

There was nothing out of the ordinary on the fridge door, just the usual memos he'd left for himself, stickers Nina had tacked on there over the years and which would prove arduous to remove should it ever become necessary. There were postcards, *Hello Kitty* magnets, a reminder on Magnusson Enterprises stationary that the NADA convention in San Francisco was a week from Monday. There were takeout menus, grocery receipts, and unpaid bills with the due dates circled in dramatic red, but nothing that would indicate any plans he might have forgotten. There were, however, three blank rectangular spaces in the middle of the clutter, whiter than the rest of the fridge surface, which indicated that something had been removed. He had to struggle to recall if those had always been there, or if maybe whatever had been there had fallen off over time.

Troubled, but unsure why, he returned to the hall to the imitation old rotary phone on the antique mahogany stand by the front door. He dialed Nina first. His call went to voice mail.

"Hey, honey," he said, after the beep, "This is Dad. Just checking where you guys have gotten off to. I don't remember if maybe I was supposed to meet you somewhere, or...anyway, the weather's pretty rough out there so call me back as soon as you can so I don't worry, okay? Happy birthday, sweetheart. Love you. Bye."

Next, he dialed his wife's number.

This time, it rang. A split second later, Gloria Gaynor began to croon the chorus of "I Will Survive" elsewhere in the house. He recognized it as Barb's ringtone, and one he had never much cared for. Frustrated, he hung up. She had left her phone at home, and for all he knew, so had Nina. Perhaps his daughter's phone was dead. The thought that followed quickly on the heels of this made him feel as if the snow had somehow found its way inside his guts.

Perhaps she is too.

3

Another hour passed, and now he was convinced something was wrong. They would never have gone somewhere this long, not on his daughter's birthday, not without leaving him a message, or without taking their phones so they could call him. Even if they'd forgotten the phones at home, they'd still have reached him from wherever they'd ended up.

He began to pace, began to war with panic.

He looked out the kitchen window. The snowfall was worsening. Images assailed him of car wrecks and blinking red lights, of smoke and fire and broken glass and blood in the snow, of hot engines hissing as they cooled, of twisted metal, pale flesh growing paler, of officious looking men in uniforms darkening the glass of his front door, of bad news, of grief, of horror...of horror...

He stopped and put his hands to his face.

Stop it. Stop it, for God's sake. They're fine.

Of course they were. Of course. Any minute now, a car would turn into the driveway he had shoveled clear for them, and they would bluster into the hall all breathless from the cold and the excitement. Barb would have the cake under her arm; Nina would feign indifference, which the twinkle in her eyes would belie. And they would look at him oddly, registering the worry, and poke fun at him, and everything would be all right. They would sit and have cake—red velvet, Nina's favorite—and he would feel like a fool for ever thinking anything was wrong.

He nodded, attempted a smile. It didn't last.

Something *was* wrong. He could feel it.

On a fine summer afternoon when the light lasted longer, he might have been able to persuade himself that he was being ridiculous, frantic for no good reason at all. But today, with the fishbelly sky getting darker by the second, it felt as if a giant cold fist had tightened itself around the house, trapping him inside, holding him there so he had no chance to escape the nightmare that was relentlessly bearing down upon him.

Jessica, he thought and felt a flare of hope blossom through the cold. *Barb's friend will know if they made other plans.* He returned to the phone, dialed his wife's number and waited a few beats for her phone to ring. Then he set down the receiver and followed Gloria Gaynor's voice to the upstairs bedroom, trying to stay composed as he entered the room he had—but for that three-month dark period two years ago—shared with Barb for the past twenty-one years.

His heart took a jolt and he froze in the doorway.

Her cell phone was on the floor. Gloria Gaynor's chorus ran out only to loop again.

Don't overreact.

There was, he told himself, any number of innocuous reasons why his wife's cell phone might be on the floor instead of on her person or plugged in to charge, the likeliest scenario being that it simply fell out of her purse while she was hustling to leave...for what? To go where? There was absolutely no reason that just the sight of the phone lying there untended and forgotten indicated SIGNS OF A STRUGGLE, four words that tried to flash like a faulty neon sign behind his eyes every time he blinked. He scooped up the phone, swiped a finger across the screen to access it, and was met with a lock screen, one which required him to enter a code to proceed further. As he struggled to remember what the code might be, or to remember if he had ever known it, Gloria Gaynor's maddening chorus died and so did the phone.

"Christ." He sat down on the bed and looked around the room. Everything was as it should be other than that stupid out-of-place phone. Had there been a struggle, surely more than that would seem off kilter. He struggled to calm himself, an effort that did not extend to his trembling fingers and headed back downstairs.

4

Something's wrong. Something's wrong. Something's wrong.

Another hour and full dark had fallen.

Callum paced the house from room to room, terrified, demanding that by some miracle they occupy themselves and cure him of the terrible crawling horror that was filling him up inside. He knew how preposterous an idea it seemed to call the police, but really, was it all that crazy on a day like today, with the weather whipping itself into a howling storm in which no living soul was welcome or safe? And on his daughter's birthday? A day in which they had no business being anyplace else but here?

Any minute now, he reassured himself. *Any minute now they'll be home and all my panicking will be for nothing.*

But he no longer believed that to be true. They were gone, maybe lost, maybe hurt, maybe dead, but they weren't here at home and that could only mean the worst.

Someone broke in. Someone broke in and took them.

There was no indication that that was the case, and his wife's discarded phone was not what anyone other than a crazy man would consider compelling evidence.

They left you. Lit out for the territories while you were at work.

This was the most ridiculous notion of all. Even if they had secretly and expertly been plotting to leave him, and even if somehow, he'd been blissfully unaware of their unhappiness and plans to mutiny the H.M.S. Callum, everything they owned was still here.

Except those pictures on the fridge.

He shook his pounding head and headed for Nina's room. Nobody could build a new life on a handful of pictures.

They were in an accident.

The worst and most plausible scenario. But if so, then why had no one called him to notify him?

Because they haven't yet identified the bodies.

Oh Jesus...

He shoved his way past the signs on Nina's door forbidding him entry and sat down at her desk and her laptop computer. Maybe if he could access it, he might see some indication of what she and her mother had been planning today. He didn't quite know what he expected to find: secret correspondence with some distant uncle who had agreed to shelter them from Callum as a result of his...what, neglect? Or maybe invitations to that party somewhere in town he had somehow managed to forget. It lessened the terror a little to imagine that at the end of all this, the worst thing he might end up having to deal with would be a family irked at his failure to recall where the festivities had been scheduled to take place.

He opened the laptop, tapped the space bar and waited.

If he found nothing here, he knew the only action left to him, no matter how crazy it seemed, would be to call the police. He wouldn't be hysterical. He'd simply express his concerns that his wife and daughter were not at home long after they should have been, and given the weather outside, he'd felt it best to check to make sure they hadn't had car trouble. *Could you please send out a patrol car to check?* Yes, that would be the way to go.

And if they find something?

He couldn't think about that. Not now. Not again.

Nina's computer screen blinked to life, a goldfish icon grinning at him above a request for her password.

Which of course, he didn't know.

"*Goddammit.*" He slammed a hand down on the laptop hard enough to send an empty water glass rimmed with Nina's lip gloss tumbling into her wastepaper basket. Quaking, heart pounding hard enough to hurt, he leaned over to retrieve it.

It was here he found the photographs that, up until this morning, had hung upon the fridge.

5

He spoke with his face pressed to the wall beside the door of Nina's room.

"Delaware County Sherriff's Department."

He cleared his throat. "Yes, I'm not sure who I need to talk to, or if I'm overreacting, but I'm concerned about my wife and daughter. I think they're out in the storm and they should have been back hours ago. It's my daughter's birthday."

"Okay. What is your name, sir?"

"Callum Dover."

"And your address?"

"158 Larchmont Terrace."

"Okay, just one moment, sir."

"Thank you."

The house had become a storm at sea, the walls shuddering and creaking around him, the hissing of the wind and snow like sea spray against the windows. If ever there was an omen that something was wrong, surely this was it. Even had he chosen to ignore such blatant natural signs that things had gone awry, he could feel it in his bones.

"Sir?"

"Yes, I'm here."

"I apologize; the line is bad."

Despite the storm, Callum didn't hear any sign of interference on the line at all. "Okay."

"Can you give me your name and address again, please?"

He did. "They've been gone for hours. I expected them to be home when I got here, but there's nobody—"

"You said 158 Larchmont Terrace?"

"Yes Ma'am. Why are—?"

"And the zip code there?"

Callum frowned. "The zip? It's 43252. You're right up the block from me."

"And where are you calling me from now, sir?"

"For God's sakes, I'm calling you from *home*."

"I'm just double-checking. And how long have you lived in that house, sir?"

Callum ran a hand over his face. "I'm sorry? I don't understand why you're asking me these questions?"

"Because you said you live at 158 Larchmont Terrace, is that correct?"

"For the umpteenth time, *yes*."

"Well, that's not where you're calling me from, sir."

Light and shadow swept across Callum's face as a car's headlights filled the downstairs windows. "Oh, thank Christ."

"Sir?"

Voices giggling. Car doors slamming. Shadows in the headlights, heading for the door. The garage door whirring open, all barely audible over the storm, but all most certainly there. Callum thought he might collapse from the relief.

"Sir?"

"Yeah, false alarm," he said into the phone. "Thanks for nothing." And hung up.

He hurried down the stairs, fear making way for the upset that they had made him wait so long with nary a word and a mild irritation that they had excluded him from their fun. But none of that was worth harping on about now. It was okay, and nothing was wrong. His family had been returned to him. Safe.

The front door opened and two figures clad in heavy parkas, one taller than the other, hurried into the hall on the trail of some shared joke.

"I'm freezing," one of them said, and whipped down her hood as her mother turned on the hallway light.

Callum froze.

The daughter saw him and jerked backward, colliding with the door and shutting it on a third party, who laughed and thumped his fist against the wood. "Hey, not funny, honey."

Two of the three faces from the photographs he had removed from the fridge stared up at him in terror. Faces he didn't know.

"Who are you?" the mother asked, panicked, clutching her daughter protectively to her side. "What are you doing in our house?"

The knocking on the door subsided and they moved away from the door, which opened to admit a gust of snow-laden wind and a large black man in a heavy jacket. "Honey, can you believe some asshole parked his car in our gara—" His smile vanished as he looked from the terror on his wife's face to the cause of it still frozen on the stairs.

"Who the fuck are you?" The big man moved to shield his family, his stance aggressive, hostile.

Territorial.

"May I...may I just get my wife's phone and be on my way?" Callum asked. "She'll need it when she comes home."

"Call the police," the big man said, and his wife hurried away into the darkness of the house. "Sarah," he said to his daughter, "Honey, get my golf club."

And Callum, who had been waiting with so much hope for so many years in so many homes for his family to come back to him, began to sob.

THE QUIET

I AM NOT DEAF.
I am not dumb.
There are just things I can't say because my voice has been stolen.

The luxury of hearing the voices of others has been denied me. It's a punishment, and one that perfectly fits the crime.

I sit and watch television and hear everything the cathode shoots against the glass. I can hear the house creaking beneath the weight of the snow. I can hear the squirrels chattering in the attic and rolling empty walnut shells across the floor. I can hear my wife puttering around the kitchen in an attempt to avoid my room, to avoid *me*. Memory tells me she hums while she cooks, but it may only *be* a memory. Things have changed. The house is always cold. It didn't use to be, but then we used to have a son to warm it.

It's been cold since I killed him.

* * *

It started with a silly argument, one that would most likely have been forgotten later, if there had been a later for Bryan.

Or maybe it wouldn't have been dismissed so easily.

I can remember hating my parents, but not why, except maybe because I felt as if they were everywhere, standing in all four corners of that room in my head, and whispering advice I thought I didn't need. They suffocated me with love and concern, and when you're a teenager, toeing the line into adulthood, that's almost as bad as waking up to find them standing over you, in the dark, with pillows in their hands and horrible smiles on their faces.

I made a promise that I would never be that way with my kid.

It didn't work.

I didn't have the words to explain to him why we never really felt the bond every father and son is supposed to have, why our conversations invariably ended in tension and left us exhausted from shouting at one another. But I was good at anger, had a quick temper, and Bryan knew it, seemed to delight in drawing it out so I'd feel impotent and guilty afterward. Or maybe I'm misdirecting now that he's not here to answer for it. Maybe it was just me.

If only we'd known that night that the argument was to be our last, we might have reached for the frayed strands of reason instead of beating at each other's skulls with testosterone hammers.

The first volley was fired as we turned off a dirt road onto the highway that would lead us home. The bags of groceries we'd picked up from the store were pale shapes crouching in the rearview, their white plastic surfaces streaked by the shadows of the rain on the windows.

"Can't see a damn thing out there," I remarked. "Nights like this, you could be up a deer's behind before you even saw the antlers. Guess we should have listened to your mother. Woman should be working for The Weather Channel."

Bryan was sitting in the passenger seat, arms folded tightly across the chest of his gabardine jacket in a classic defensive pose. The jacket was as ill-fitting as the small smirk on his face. He hadn't spoken to me since the store, since I'd refused to buy him cigarettes after the clerk demanded to see his ID. He was not yet eighteen. He would be soon, but I wasn't going to jump the gun on that score and didn't advocate his doing it either, though I was not naïve enough to think he hadn't already gone a few rounds with life and come away with the scars to prove it.

The silence stretched between us until it was almost unbearable. I heard him sigh, saw him reach for the stereo and started to say something, but he beat me to it. "Went to the recruitment center yesterday. Me and Todd." I saw then, as my guts turned cold at his words, that he hadn't been reaching for the stereo after all, but the cigarette lighter next to it, which he thumbed in before sitting back to look out the window.

I kept my eyes on the road as the headlights knifed through the belly of the rainswept night. I could feel his smirk growing and my fear quickly turned ugly, turned to anger. "For what?"

"What do you mean: 'for what'?" A six-pack and some porn. The fuck you think we went there for?"

Hearing that, I should have told him to watch his language, as per the instructions in the Good Parenting Handbook. His mother would have. But seeing him turn into a shadow of myself at his age scared me more than that old image of my parents with their murderous pillows. And worse, I felt like the one holding that pillow now. But reason, despite its reputation for prevailing between two intelligent people, completely deserted me in that moment. It was overruled by dread.

I searched the night for words, read the signs that swept blurrily past the windshield, and said the only thing I could think of: "I thought you were done with that stuff, Bryan. I thought you got it out of your system. Didn't we discuss this? Didn't we talk about—?"

"Last time we talked," he interrupted, "You were the one doing all the talking."

The sigh that came rushing out of me had a hundred words I had the good sense not to voice, like poisonous fish being swept away in a current. From the corner of my eye I saw him withdraw from his breast pocket a badly crumpled pack of Marlboros. He flipped it open and drew out a cigarette with his teeth, an irritating and relatively new habit he'd acquired somewhere, probably from Todd, his malcontent friend. My grip on the steering wheel grew tighter. "Light that," I said through clenched teeth, "And you'll follow it out the window."

He snatched the cigarette from his lips. "Christ almighty."

I glared at him, and that good sense finally abandoned me. "Watch your goddamn mouth. You may think you're king of the hill, kid, but you're not yet past the age where I won't give you a fat lip."

"Oh yeah? Well...I'll be eighteen in two months," he declared, "so you'd better get used to treating me like an adult."

"You want to be treated like an adult?"

"It's what I said, isn't it?"

"Then start acting like one. This petulant poor-me crap is getting old."

He scoffed. "Whatever." With a shrug, he tucked the near-empty Marlboro pack back into his pocket, but kept the cigarette clenched between his fingers. After a dramatic sigh, he gave me a withering look that, God help me, made me want to punch him in the mouth, something my old man would have done without pause for thought. I guess knowing that kept me in check. The muscle in my jaw quivered.

"What's with this whole rebellion thing anyway?" I asked. "If you'd had it rough, I guess I'd understand, but your mom and I have given you a pretty good life. So why the attitude?"

He didn't answer. Instead, he rolled the cigarette over and between his fingers like a grifter with a coin.

A car, dangerously close, its lights filling my windshield, honked in protest and I brought my focus back to the road. I'd let the Taurus drift a little over the centerline and now I straightened it out with the silent admonition that nothing would ever get resolved between us if I drove the car into a semi. Not that I had much hope for resolution anyway. For that, he'd have to be open to such a thing, and at that moment, he looked like a padlocked door.

"I don't get it," I said. "I don't get what it is you're trying to prove, or to whom you're trying to prove it."

"I know you don't," he said.

"So, enlighten me."

"I signed up. I'm joining the army. No big deal. *You* were in the service, so why are you asking me to explain?"

"Because I thought I told you enough stories to make sure you'd never consider it as a career. Stories about what I *saw* in 'Nam. So, if you're doing it to get back at me for whatever it is you think I've done, then there are much better, much more sensible ways to do it. Ways that won't lead you by the hand straight into a hell you're not ready for."

"I'm doing it because I want to. Not because of you. Don't flatter yourself."

"And what do you think the army will do for you?"

He pondered the question for a moment, then leaned his head back against the headrest and shrugged. "Dunno. Teach me a few things I can't learn on my own. And besides, things have changed since you served. The way it goes these days, I'll probably end up getting paid for mending fences at some military outpost that never sees any action."

I chuckled without humor. "Keep telling yourself that, kid. I'm sure all those boys over in Iraq thought the same thing."

"Spare me," Bryan said.

I frowned, took my eyes off the road long enough to study him. "Bryan, that's one line you'll find real goddamn effective when you're up to your ass in sand with some Taliban lunatic pointing a rifle at your head."

He smiled, and it was an ugly thing to behold. "I can handle myself. There are fools out there with busted noses who can testify to that."

"Yeah, I'm sure," I said, knowing it wasn't true, knowing too how desperately he wanted to believe it was.

We fell silent again, the rain drumming on the roof and the squeak-thump laboring of the wipers filling the void.

I wanted to throttle him. So help me, I wanted to pull the car over, drag his sour, sulky ass out of the car and beat seven shades of shit out of him in the hope that it would leave enough room for the sense to gain a foothold. The army. For fuck sake, it had been my life, had almost been the end of it more than once. I still had nightmares. Still flinched when a car backfired. Still felt my gorge rise at the sight or scent of blood. It had not been a life for a kid. I didn't want it to be Bryan's life, now or ever. But how to make him understand that? He had something to prove, not to me, or anyone else, but to himself. Was it even right to try and stop it? Probably not, but I wanted to so bad it hurt. How to explain to him what the army had been to me. How it had been such a part of my life, everything else had seemed secondary, how dreams of past victories gave way to nightmares populated by friends who had ended up as dark stains on my uniform or unidentifiable body parts half sunk in the mud. How to tell him that they came back for me, those men, my friends, who I'd led into Hell, and they took their place as ghosts haunting the house inside my head.

"When you were a kid," I said. "You asked me about 'Nam. You remember that?"

He rubbed his eyes and groaned. "Can we not do this now?"

I ignored him and continued, because I had to. I felt as if I were being given this one last shot at reclaiming him as my son. One last chance to save him. If I didn't, I'd lose him forever. "You remember asking me about all those guys in the photographs in the shoebox under my bed? I got mad because you went snooping and found them."

He didn't respond, but I knew he was listening.

"I don't want them there, Bryan. I don't like being in bed chasing sleep and knowing their faces are under there, in the dark, but I can't get rid of them. Can't throw them away. Can't even move them. You know why? Because as long as they're there, they know I'm not forgetting them, or trying to. I stick them in the back of a closet somewhere and it's like I'm trying to hide them, like it's a secret I'm ashamed of. I do that, the nightmares will get worse." To my dismay I felt my throat tighten, choking off a sudden involuntary sob. I gave it a moment, swallowed, and continued. "I get scared that if I did get rid of them, they might come back for real, to make sure I remembered in stark detail every single one of their deaths, and my part in them." I fell silent for fear of saying what I'd just been thinking, something that if said aloud wouldn't have changed anything despite it being the absolute truth: *I don't want to have to sleep in that bed some night above your picture, Bryan. I don't want you down there in the dark staring up at me, blaming me for not saving you.*

"That's sad and all," my son said, "but you already said you don't understand, and all you're doing now is proving it. Like I said, it's different now. So quit trying to get it when you obviously can't."

At his complete lack of empathy, I felt sudden heat sear the inside of my chest and my hands tensed on the wheel until the rubber creaked. "I don't get it? That's priceless, Bryan. Really. I've been through the kind of Hell you and your spoiled, self-entitled generation have only seen in the movies or on the news. I fucking *lived* through it, but you think, at *seventeen years of age*, that you have it all figured out, huh?" I shook my head in disgust. "You think you're going to enlist, spend some time trading salutes, scrubbing floors, maybe get to fire off a few rounds and then come home to a parade? Is that what you think it is? Well I hate to burst your bubble, but chances are you'll be put right out there on the firing line watching your friends get killed and, if you're lucky, and you manage not to get shot to shit or lose some body parts, it's where you'll stay. That life is a lottery, Bryan, and if you don't win, you die, or end up wishing you had." I slapped my hand hard against the steering wheel. "But hey, what do I know, right? You obviously know more about it than I do, so why bother trying to argue with you? Stubborn sonofabitch."

Yes, he was stubborn. As stubborn as *I'd* made him. As stubborn as I had been at his age. It was a dumb argument and even then, I knew it. Every word I spoke might as well have come from my own father's mouth, so inescapable was his influence no matter how much I abhorred it. But I'd remembered and retained every lecture he'd ever given me, just as I was sure Bryan would remember mine. After he'd learned the truth his own way. The hard way. After it was too late to do anything but blame me for being right.

"Anyway," he said, screwing the cigarette between his lips and prodding the lighter in again. "You're not arguing with me. You're telling me how to live my life, which is rich considering the balls you've made of your own."

There was one feeble scream of protest from somewhere inside me, perhaps from one of those ghosts wandering the old, rotten hallways in my head, but it was too quiet and too late to be heeded. The rage rose like a thing independent of me, and before I could stop myself, I thrust out my arm and backhanded my son across the face. Hard. The cigarette flew from his mouth and he jerked away, shock already replacing his typically dour expression as he looked down at the darkness between his feet and brought a trembling hand to his lip. Blood welled. Not much, but enough. It was the first and only time I'd ever hit him, and immediately I regretted it, hated myself for it. But there was no taking it back or excusing it, and no words with which to do so even if I tried.

Apologize. Say something. Now, before it's too late.

It already was.

Cigarette lost somewhere under his seat, Bryan produced the pack of Marlboros. Still trembling, his dark hair hanging in his face, he flipped the top open and bit down on the filter of his last smoke. I almost smiled as he yanked the lighter free from his pocket and lit up.

Apologize. There's still time.

Determined to try, no matter how useless it might ultimately end up being, I opened my mouth, breath shuddering out of me, but it was Bryan's voice that shattered the quiet. "DAD!"

A red glare flooded the windshield as if we'd driven into a fire. Confusion hit me between the eyes almost like a backhanded slap from a desperate father.

A car had stopped dead in the middle of the road. I caught the briefest glimpse of what looked like a man in a yellow slicker staggering drunkenly off the side of the road before I wrenched the wheel hard to the left. Bryan cried out. I reached for him as the car sailed off the road, plowing us into a telephone pole with bone-shattering abruptness.

Neither one of us had been wearing our seatbelts. The impact drove the steering wheel toward me with the force of a freight train, making bone meal of my chest even as the impetus tried to force my body forward. My legs, caught beneath a steering column that was accordioning in on itself, twisted and broke and I felt a fiery pain shoot up my back. There was nothing to do, but sit and bounce around like a marionette, convinced I was being rent asunder amid a chorus of shattering glass and screeching metal. It seemed to last forever. My eyes, flickering and dimming out of focus, narrowed instinctively against the blizzard of flying glass and broken plastic, but not before seeing Bryan traveling headfirst through the windshield into the telephone pole and back down onto the crumpled hood. The rain turned crimson.

"Bry—" I tried to say through clenched teeth and was shoved back into my seat so suddenly and violently that I broke my neck and several vertebrae, though of course I would not learn this until later, when none of it would matter. The pain asserted itself then, alternating between hot and cold hammer strikes to my spine and skull. I grunted and closed my eyes, trying not to see my son lying on the hood, his face inches away from where I sat unable to move, unable to reach out and touch what remained of his head. The car slammed down on its wheels and began to roll slowly backward. Glass tinkled; steam hissed; metal groaned. The only human sounds were my own as I wept and coughed up blood.

Bryan still held the cigarette between his broken fingers. As I watched, the miraculously still-lit cherry went out with a small hiss in a narrow stream of his blood.

Before I lost consciousness, I heard someone laugh, then a woman screaming for someone to call 911. It sounded like a sensible but pointless idea. My son was dead. I was going to stay with him, and if there was any mercy or justice, I would join him.

But I didn't, because there isn't. I merely slept and waited to be repaired and set back on the monotonous track of a life I no longer deserved.

* * *

Winter came, as harsh as grief. The earth grew icy teeth; the ground froze. Ice storms made for difficult hospital visits. And snow fell endlessly, whispering rapturously of autumn's death. The cold clambered at the house, huffed at the sills, trying to find a way in. It needn't have bothered. It was plenty cold inside.

In the months after Bryan's death, I came to understand that the "for better or for worse" part of marriage vows doesn't cover filicide, and that no matter how well you think you know someone, they can still surprise you.

I tried very hard to hate Estelle for shutting me out, for looking at me like some cheap replacement of her husband, a replacement that required little affection and even less attention save the tasks she had no choice but to fulfill, or risk becoming a murderer herself. But I couldn't. When you hate yourself and begrudge your lungs every breath, how can you hate anyone who has to live with it? Did I deserve the accusation, the blame for our son's death, that capered in her eyes every time she looked at me? Maybe. Maybe not. I've gone over and back on that more times than I can count. Arguments for and against can be made ad nauseum. A popular one was that I had killed our son long before I crashed the car. I'd shut him out, failed to understand him, and God, or cosmic justice, or karma, or whatever it is that exists beyond the veil that so frequently tries to suffocate us, gave me a taste of my own medicine, forcing me in turn to try to comprehend the mechanics of a cruel, hostile universe that made no sense without Bryan as its sun.

I couldn't fight the guilt, didn't want to. Instead, I retreated into myself, occasionally surfacing to respond to Estelle's dutiful and perfunctory attempts at conversation. These occasions were few and far between, the distance between us growing greater each time, and invariably I was left out in the cold once more.

We were no longer husband and wife, but patient and nurse.

In the mirror, I saw a gray-haired man in a wheelchair, a stranger upon whose palsied frame, wrinkled clothes hung like rags on a scarecrow. I stared at that unshaven creature with the dead eyes, the creature Estelle faced every day, and I understood how easy I had made it for her to forget the man she had married, had once loved. To her, I was as much a ghost as our son, and while she might have had other suggestions for the kind of box in which I belonged, I knew I'd condemned myself to the one that waited in the dark beneath our bed.

I was a murderer.

I had nothing left to lose.

Or so I thought.

* * *

Early in December, the festive season encroaching on every house but ours. A single sad-looking wreath on the front door was Estelle's sole concession to celebration. Ghosts, after all, have little to celebrate, and the living have too much to mourn.

I awoke, warm in bed, enjoying the brief strains of peaceful ignorance that greets even the most broken upon first waking, and I looked up at the bedroom ceiling, specifically at a gathering of ladybugs. They were an industrious little crew, mapping out the terrain, embarking on furtive missions, and nestling themselves in the cracks in the plaster, all of them united in the critical pursuit of warmth. They were like flecks of blood on fresh snow; red ink on a white page.

I heard footsteps on the stairs and a moment later Estelle appeared in the doorway. I offered her a smile and went back to watching the red horde on the ceiling. If I concentrated, I could hear them, their legs ticking against the ceiling, their carapaces sliding together, wings buzzing.

Estelle's shadow sprawled across my face and did not move.

The ladybugs began to form a pattern, roughly heart-shaped. Perhaps even insects have a sense of tragic irony.

Abruptly, Estelle grabbed my wrist as if she were trying to wrench my arm out of its socket. Startled, I looked questioningly at her, only to see the same expression on her drawn, haggard face. A face that once, not so long ago, had been so beautiful, so radiant, before I robbed her of the one thing that had lit us both from within.

Her mouth moved.

I shook my head in confusion.

There were no words.

"Estelle, stop..."

She frowned, angry, and shook me. Panic beat a tattoo in my chest. Her mouth formed words that did not make it to my ears. Had I gone deaf?

Tick-tick-tick. No, I could hear the slight scratch of the ladybugs, the drip-drip-dripping of the faucet in the bathroom, the radio playing downstairs. No, not deaf. Then what? Was she playing some kind of game?

She leaned close. I could smell her perfume and the vestiges of smoke from cigarettes she'd quit before Bryan died. Her brown eyes probed mine, poking inside my skull, looking for a reason, any reason why she shouldn't just grab a pillow and end our mutual suffering here and now.

"I can't hear you, honey," I told her, but her eyes grew hooded. She hadn't heard. *Couldn't* hear me, my words as soundless to her as hers were to me. She straightened, cast me a look so full of contempt that it made my skin crawl, and stormed out of the room. *One more thing*, that look had said. *Just one more fucking punishment.*

Dread seized me, but only for a moment. I returned my gaze to the bugs and watched them until my heart stopped thundering, stopped hurting, until it dawned on me that I was a fool to be surprised by this latest hellish development. Hadn't I expected this, or if not this, then *something?* Isn't that the lot for those of us who dwell in Hell? Whomever or whatever controlled my fate now had opted to chip further away at my resolve, to take away every basic function until there was nothing left but a twisted wretch in a tattered robe with nothing left to do but wait to die.

* * *

I slept and dreamed of faceless soldiers standing on the lip of a crumbling trench, their shadows pinning Bryan and me to the muddy earth down below, where we struggled not to drown in the yellow water. But we dared not raise our heads, dared not let the enemy know we were still alive lest they feel immediately compelled to rectify their error. When they were gone, I sat up, and realized I'd been holding my son beneath the water to hide him.

And that I had held him down for far too long.

* * *

In the coming weeks there were doctors, and more doctors, and specialists and suits who didn't seem to think it necessary to let me know who or what they were. Which was fine. I was beyond caring anyway. In fact, I admit to deriving a certain degree of pleasure from their bafflement and consternation, their soundless pontificating and theorizing. They paced and pondered, poked and prodded, and stared at me as if waiting for me to drop the charade. The activity was something of a relief, a reprieve from the banal. Strangers drifted into my room, their coattails whispering, their expensive shoes making dull, urgent thumps against the shag carpet. Clinically detached faces peered down at me, suspicion in their eyes, and made clinically detached observations. Lights burned my eyes, tubes were snaked into my body. I was monitored relentlessly.

They tried to teach me to talk, as if I had simply forgotten how, and when that failed, they aimed their professional smiles my way and tried to instruct me on how to communicate via other means: coded blinks, expressions, lip movements. How I wished for the use of my fingers, however briefly, so I could offer them the universal one-fingered symbol of rejection. A girl came to read my lips and what I told her made her blush and apologize to Estelle, who looked at me with even less favor than before.

Still, they persisted.

They shoved a pen in my mouth and slid paper before my face, then gathered around me like vultures waiting for carrion. I let them starve, occupying my time and wasting theirs by doodling and drawing cartoonish representations of their irritation, as well as other, less pleasant things. And through it all, Estelle sat in the hall and smoked, or stood in the doorway impassive as a cigar-store Indian.

I started seeing less and less of her.

I started seeing less and less of the doctors.

Then one morning I woke up and the machines were gone, and so were they.

* * *

Some days later, Estelle came to see me, and I knew by the look on her face and the tears in her eyes, that it would be the last time. I knew, and for the first time I blessed whatever medical anomaly or mental breakdown had robbed me of the ability to hear voices.

But my wife was nothing if not creative.

In her left hand she held a small black tape recorder. She took my hand and began to weep. I wondered what those tears meant as I slowly looked away, afraid I'd freeze and shatter into a thousand pieces if I stared too long at the cold in her eyes. So, I watched the bugs and told myself she was regretful, remembering the happier times we'd shared.

But I didn't believe that. Reason suggested she was crying for herself, mourning a life she would never get back, even after she left her crippled, silent husband. Still, I like to think at least some of those tears were for me and the love that had once bound us together.

With the snow falling softly outside the window behind her, she spoke slowly enough that I could read her lips. "I'm sorry."

I offered her an understanding smile that must have been grotesque if it looked anything like it felt. She set the tape recorder down on my chest. There was not much weight to it, but she might as well have placed a headstone there.

Estelle clicked the PLAY button, bent low and kissed my forehead, then turned and left me to listen to the static crackle and whirr of the tape running toward her voice. I closed my eyes and bit my lower lip until it bled.

A theory I'd formulated was proven correct as Estelle's voice filled the room, and my ears.

I can only hear voices when they're transmitted through an electronic medium—the phone, the television...a tape recorder.

Curious, I suppose, but inconsequential in the grand scheme of things.

The tape recorder squeaked and hummed as the little wheels turned in the small glass window.

The ladybugs ceased their wandering and grew blurry.

I listened for what felt like an hour as my wife explained why she hated me, how she couldn't go on living with another ghost that did nothing but remind her of her dead son. She ended by letting me know she was not leaving me to die, that a nurse was coming to tend to me in her absence until better, more permanent arrangements could be made. *You are not*, she told me, *being abandoned.*

She still loved me, she said, but I reminded her of death.

Her words echoed long after the tape had clicked to a stop.

I have always loved the sound of her voice.

* * *

Nurse Dobson was a large black woman and so damn congenial that I promptly abandoned my initial efforts to drive her insane. Every hour of every day she'd come to me, fluff my pillows, change the bedpan, water the ferns, sit and chit-chat...and through it all, that smile of hers never wavered. In the face of such indomitable cheer, it was inevitable, despite all I'd been through and what might yet lay ahead, that we would become friends. And we did. I knew little about her home life other than the occasional tidbits she chose to share, but I found myself guessing that she wasn't accustomed to being listened to, which of course made me her ideal patient. She spoke at length about her past, her dreams and ambitions, and I said nothing, just listened.

Which of course, was what I should have been doing all along.

Listening.

It took a while for Nurse Dobson to understand what I required of her, but at last that smile of hers changed from confusion to realization. She nodded her assent and went to fetch the tape recorder. I wasn't sure it would work, but I had hope. After all, if I could hear voices through the machine, maybe the recorder could pick up *my* voice, even when it seemed as if there was nothing to record. It was worth a shot. The fact that it did made me think of the doctors and their endless tests and I almost laughed. I won't pretend to understand any of this myself, and I don't much care how or why it worked, only that it did.

And so I sat in my wheelchair, the tape recorder on my lap set to RECORD, looking out the window at a world that seemed eternally white, the twisted limbs of the walnut trees bowing in deference to the weight of winter, and I began to tell my story, unsure who might eventually hear it, uncertain who might care, but it seemed important that someone, if only Nurse Robson, if only the room, understand that in the end, I saw the light.

I am not deaf.

I am not dumb.

There are just things I can't say because my voice has been stolen.

The luxury of hearing the voices of others has been denied me. It's a punishment, and one that perfectly fits the crime

Because I didn't listen when I had the chance. Until now, I haven't been listening hard enough to what the quiet has been trying to tell me. With words and voices removed, I can finally hear what I was meant to hear. The whispers of truth are coming from this room, from the shadowy corners where there stands a boy, his head bowed, teeth bared as he nips the filter on a cigarette and draws it ever so slowly upward. I can't see his free hand. It's hidden in the thickest of the shadows. I wonder if he's holding a pillow behind his back, or perhaps that's me being silly and superimposing onto him ideas of the kind of fate I think I deserve. Like so many things, it hardly matters now.

As his reflection, pale as snow, moves into place beside my own in the window glass, he's smiling, and I can hear him clearly when he speaks.

He can hear me too, and that is good.

We have so much to discuss.

THEY KNOW

THE PHONE RINGS JUST AS THE WEEPING STOPS. *He stares at the glass and the amber panacea within, shutting out the trilling with minimal effort. There is nothing to hear. Just as there was nothing to hear the last time he answered the phone. Nothing but damnable winter breathing on the line and the faintest whisper, whispering the impossible: "They know."*
Just the wind.
And the ticking from the walls of the deathwatch winding down.

* * *

Snow.

Jake Dodds was so very tired of it.

It seemed winter had crept in while he was sleeping, draping drop cloths over the town of Miriam's Cove and hushing itself with guilty whispers.

It was everywhere, layered on the ground, hunched over the hedgerows in the garden, bowing the branches of the trees in the yard, shotgun blasts of it on the sides of cars and windows, fired by children driven by manic excitement. It was on the roofs, the sills, the shoulders of people ducking to avoid the sharp wind that sent it flurrying into their grimacing faces.

Everywhere.

And it didn't seem as if it would ever stop. It didn't seem as if the underlying vibrant green luster of life would ever return. Even the sun had been reduced to a foggy white cyst beneath the pale skin of the sky.

He was starting to feel as if the whole goddamn season, with its twinkling lights and carols, dazzling storefronts and endless slew of commercials advertising mind-numbing electric toys, was to blame for the snow. People expected snow for Christmas and maybe the collective power of that expectation was enough to make it so. Whatever the reason, he didn't like it one bit. Christmas was a time for sitting around the fire eating marshmallows and fruit cake, for decorating the tree with loved ones and maybe indulging in a snifter of brandy before bed, for gifts that meant something and for the excited chatter of children when they discovered the bounty beneath the tree.

But now, six days before Christmas, sitting by his window and staring out at an almost monochrome world, Jake realized that all that was gone, not only in the minds of the masses, but from his own life too.

A distinct awareness of family values and a fondness for the ritualistic aspect of the season had not been enough to keep his wife alive or his children from growing up and scattering themselves around the world. Leaving him alone with the white and an empty house to watch it from.

Clearing the condensation away with a swipe of his hand, he scowled at the silent fall of snow as children giggled and flung handfuls of the stuff at each other.

In his garden stood a long-suffering walnut tree, a beard of white nestled in its crotch almost like mimicry of the season's patron saint.

Jake thought he knew what it felt like to be that tree – immobile, rooted to the ground, trapped and powerless to do anything but stand by and watch the passage of time, unable to run away from the grief, the sorrow and all the dark things that sharpened the edges of life.

He shook his head, sliding the cover over the well from which such melodrama sprung and allowed himself the faintest hint of a smile as a tall, wiry figure in a brown suit and overcoat appeared, ducked his head against the snow and turned the corner into Jake's driveway.

A visitor was just what he needed now, and visitors were seldom more welcome than Lenny Quick.

Jake groaned at the ache in his bones as he rose from the seat by the window, and he took a moment to steady himself before making his way to the front door.

"God's dandruff," Lenny said, snapping his hat against the palm of his hand. He inspected the hallway as if he'd never seen it before (though he had been here at least once every week for the last thirty years—except for that time in early '90 when pneumonia kept him in a hospital bed) before he turned to watch Jake shutting the soft white world outside.

"No end to it, is there?" Jake said, smiling now. Ever since Julia's death, he had felt as if the walls were closing in around him, that somewhere beyond the rose-patterned wallpaper, a clock was ticking. He heard it at night, faint but most definitely there. *Tick-tick-tick*, the winding down of his own deathwatch. Company helped silence that sound and made the ghosts nothing but tricks of light and shadow.

Lenny shivered and brushed the snow from his shoulders. "It's supposed to get a lot worse too if the weatherman is to be believed." He hung his hat atop his coat on the mahogany tree in the hall. "Saw on the news Maine's gettin' hammered, New York, same. Gonna be a bad one no matter what way you look at it. Surprised we haven't gotten more than this already, to tell the truth." He led the way into the living room, drawn by the heat. "People have been saying since the summer we're heading for the worst winter in years. Hasn't happened yet though so I reckon the bad stuff must be getting close."

Jake followed him into the living room.

A cheerful fire blazed in the fireplace, occasionally spitting sparks the fireguard caught. With Lenny here, the fire and indeed the room, looked almost cozy. Alone, the flames drew the spirit from a man and made the room seem hollow and dark.

Lenny took a seat without waiting to be asked. They had known each other too long to stand on formality. Jake moved to the sideboard beneath the window, upon which gleaming bottles stood like soldiers with immaculate uniforms, most of them empty. He tried to avoid looking at the bleached white world outside. "Usual?"

Lenny nodded and leaned forward to show his hands to the fire. "That'd be just fine. I think I'm freezing from the inside out today."

Jake poured him a brandy, a whiskey for himself.

"Thanks," Lenny said, accepting his drink. He watched Jake grimace as he lowered himself into the seat opposite. "Knees still bothering you?"

Jake nodded. "Morning, noon and night. Mornings worst of all."

"You should let a doctor take a look before you end up crawling."

"I'd *rather* crawl than see a doctor."

"Well it isn't going to get any better if you don't go see someone."

"Like who?"

"Like...I don't know, a bone man or something. Doctor Palmer would be a start."

"Nah. It'll ease up once the cold is gone."

"You sure about that?"

Jake sighed. "No. I'm not, but unless you went deaf thirty or so years ago, you should know damn well how I feel about doctors."

"Sure I do," Lenny said with a shrug, "but is a family tradition of hating doctors for no reason going to make your life any easier if this cold spell turns out to be here for the long haul?"

"We don't hate them for no reason."

Lenny smiled. "You're avoiding the question."

"I was hoping it would convince you not to pursue it."

"Have it your way, but I have a twinge of arthritis in my fingers and I have to tell you, if it hit my knees so bad I could hardly walk, I'd be spread out before Palmer like a virgin on prom night."

Jake winced. "I could have died happy without ever picturing that. Thanks."

Lenny laughed, a deep rumbling baritone and slapped his thigh. Jake grinned, but it was short-lived. Lenny wiped his eyes and when he looked up, his expression was grave.

"What is it?" Jake asked, unnerved by the intensity of his friend's stare.

Lenny waited a beat, then sipped from his glass, swishing the brandy around his mouth before he spoke. "You mentioned dying," he said, looking down into his drink. "I was wondering if you remembered the last time we talked about it. What you told me, I mean."

"Vaguely," Jake replied, too quickly, averting his eyes from Lenny's probing glare, a move he knew belied his words.

He remembered most of it and it shamed him. The snow had thickened, draining what little light had been caught dancing in the evening sky and for the gloom, he was suddenly thankful. In the firelight, the flush of color the lie had summoned to his face would go unnoticed.

It had happened two nights ago.

He staggers into the bedroom with a wail of grief and almost chokes on the breath he sucks in to power another. The shadows quickly move away from him, sliding along the walls and slipping beneath the carpet. The room ripples and sways in his tear-blurred vision, his gut full of whiskey, heart full of grief and dread. Sobbing, he drops to his knees beside the bed, repeating her name like a sacred mantra, as if it could ever be enough to raise her.

Beneath the bed—so cold, so terribly cold without her—lies a shoebox and his fingers find it fast, first feeling the sides, the lid, then clutching and dragging it out into the dull light spilling in from the hallway. Urgently, he rips the lid from the box, wipes away tears and grabs the Colt .45 in his fumbling, trembling hands.

"I hate the damn thing. Get rid of it," his wife had said the day he'd brought it home.

"It's for protection, honey. Just for protection."

"I don't like it. Bring it back. What if it goes off by mistake?"

"It won't. These things don't go off unless you mean them to."

Like I mean it to now, he thinks, and clicks back the safety. Clll-ick! He can feel the shadows around him, pressing down on him, watches held to their ears, listening. Counting off the seconds to oblivion.

In lieu of the gunshot comes a scream, a horrible guttural scream and the gun falls heavily to the floor, still wearing a bead of perspiration from his temple. He runs, runs to the phone and misdials four times before he finally hears the voice he so desperately needs to hear.

"You were pretty upset," Lenny said, looking strangely embarrassed himself, a look Jake did not see very often. "You scared the life out of me, I don't mind telling you."

"Yeah," was all Jake could think to say.

"You were going to do it too, weren't you?"

"I guess I was."

Silence then, and in it, Jake half-expected to hear a ticking. What came instead was a rattling, as the wind drove snow against the window.

"We've been friends for a long time," Lenny said, casting a half-hearted glance at the window. "Been through a lot together. I wish I was the type of guy who could advise you, but I'm not. Maybe if I'd watched more Oprah or that moronic Doctor Phil guy I'd be able to sort out all of that confusion and fear you've got gnawing away at you, but I can't." He jiggled his glass and watched the brandy lap against the sides. "I know you're lonely and hurt and scared and I keep trying to think up ways to fix that but the truth is...you've always been stronger than me, y'know? You were the one who helped me sort out my problems over the years. You were the one I turned to when my head threatened to explode with all the pressure. You were my surrogate big brother, the one I called on to slay the dragons, even if I'd never have admitted it. Too proud, you see. Now that you need help, I'm not so sure I'm any good to you, and I'm sorry for that. Truly, I am."

Jake offered him a tired smile. "You've already been good to me. I can't remember everything about that call the other night, but I do know by the time I hung up I was more terrified of that gun than anything else. If I hadn't called you..."

He left the sentence die in the air between them and nodded. "You're a good man, Lenny," he said softly and drained his glass.

Lenny leaned back from the fire, the right side of his face fading in the deepening gloom. "Nah," he said, waving away the compliment. "I was just worried my local brandy pimp'd go outta business. Where'd I be then?"

Gratitude hovered at the back of Jake's tongue but he knew vocalizing it would only embarrass Lenny. Instead, he raised his empty glass in the air and grinned. "To madmen, pimps and alcoholics," he said.

Lenny chuckled and touched his glass to Jake's. "I'll drink to that."

They both laughed until the wind thundered against the side of the house hard enough to make them both jump.

"So how are you feeling now?" Lenny asked.

"I have good and bad days. If the snow would let up or better still, vanish entirely then I wouldn't be able to count this as one of the bad ones. Goddamn snow drives me crazy."

Lenny frowned. "Why? It never bothered you before."

"I don't know. This year is different. I know it's ridiculous, but I'm a little afraid of it. Even back when the weatherman first said it was heading our way I felt apprehensive, as if he'd said a plague was coming."

"I think I'd rather have the snow," said Lenny.

"I wish I could explain it. It just feels wrong, you know? I mean, I look out that window there just like I do every other year and I see the same damn thing I always see in winter: snow and lots of it. But for some reason this year it looks less like a bunch of ice crystals and more like some kind of mold, as if the world is going stale."

Lenny stared impassively, but Jake was suddenly aware how crazy he sounded and rose from his chair before Lenny could call him on it.

"Another?" he asked, and Lenny handed him his glass.

As he refilled their drinks, he glanced out the window. The sky was darkening, slashes of silver glowing above the horizon. And still the snow fell, whipped by the wind into transparent white horses that galloped beneath the streetlights. Jake shivered.

It's growing, he thought. *That's what I was trying to tell Lenny. It looks as if it's growing, like a scab. And the street is the wound.*

He returned with the drinks and set his whiskey on the mantel while he fed the flames wood from a cast iron basket.

"Can I tell you what I think?" Lenny said.

"Sure."

"I think you need to start getting out of the house more. I'll bet you can count on one hand the amount of times you've been outside since Julia passed on."

Jake said nothing. Lenny gave a satisfied grunt.

"See? That's worse than solitary confinement. A man with the kind of worries you've got could drive himself stir crazy looking at these same four walls day in day out, especially with all the memories around here. And the snow thing? Sorry to have to tell you but I think it isn't so much the snow as the whole outside world that's got you spooked. You've become so wrapped up in your own little shell of suffering and anger—and I'm not belittling or begrudging you that; God knows Julia was one of the sweetest damn women I've ever known—that you can't bear to look beyond that window just in case it might offer you a view of a place *outside* the pain."

Jake raised his eyebrows. Lenny grinned.

"Well I'll be damned," he said, "Maybe I was wrong. *Oprah* watch out!"

"You could be right," Jake said, but he didn't think so. "But how does knowing what the problem is help any?" He rubbed a hand over his face. "I miss her, y'know?" he said quietly. "All the goddamn time. Sometimes so much I can't breathe. And at night...at night is the worst of all, when I'm asleep and I run my hand over the memory of her skin and wake to an empty bed and cold sheets. Sometimes the pain feels too real to be grief, Lenny. One night I woke up convinced I was having a heart attack. I almost called you then, too."

The fire hissed and the flames caught, restoring the warm amber glow to the room.

"You should have called me," Lenny told him. "That's what I'm there for, just like you're here to fill me with cheap brandy." He smiled but it quickly faded. "I didn't mean it to sound like I have all the answers either. I don't. I can't even imagine what this has been like for you. But I hate seeing you like this, stuck in a house alone with nothing to do but remember." He straightened in his chair and let loose an exasperated sigh. "I guess I have some titanium balls telling you how to handle things, huh?"

Jake shook his head. "No. I appreciate it. Really. I'm just tired of being afraid, you know? Tired of waking up from a nightmare only to have the real nightmare crash down around me. I feel empty, Lenny. And alone. And pretty goddamn pathetic."

"Pathetic? Why? You think two months after you lose your wife you should be all smiles and organizing house parties? The way I see it is you're handling it as good as you know how. Another man would be lying in the ground beside his wife by now after taking the chickenshit way out."

"I came close though, didn't I?"

"Yes. You did." Lenny said. "But close is still a million miles away from done and you're still here talking about it. That's good enough for me."

Jake set his glass down and rubbed his hands together. "So, what do I do?"

Lenny's face grew somber and he pointed a long, gnarled index finger at Jake's glass. "Being a bit lighter on the devil juice might help you some. I'm your friend, Jake, but if calls like that one two nights ago start getting regular, I'm buying an answering machine for Christmas."

Although Lenny chuckled to show he meant it as a joke, the point was clear. It scared Jake to think what his nights might be like without the cushioning effect of alcohol. Then again, he realized, if drinking led him to that old shoebox beneath the bed again, the next cushion might be the one in his coffin.

"You need to start finding distractions," Lenny continued. "I'm not saying you jump into a whole routine, but you could start setting aside days to go for walks. Go catch a movie every now and then. Come with me to Bingo some Friday night, see if we can't beat the pants off those Harperville hags. Hell, even stopping by to see me and the wife would be a start."

"I know, you're right, but most of those things you mentioned only remind me of who's missing from the picture."

Lenny leaned forward, his elbows resting on his knees, his hooked nose mere inches from Jake's. "It'll get easier," he said and laid a hand on Jake's shoulder. "But you have to start somewhere before you smother yourself." He stared hard into Jake's eyes, as if trying to discern something written there. "Do you understand?"

The phone rang, and Lenny sat back in his chair. "Joanne, most likely," he said, and Jake nodded as he rose, pain flaring in his knees.

"Will I tell her you're here?" he asked as he made his way out into the hall.

"Might as well," Lenny said. "She can sense it anyway."

"Still reading tea leaves?"

"Earl Grey, morning noon and night."

Jake was smiling as he picked up the phone. "Hello?"

The voice on the other end of the line was gruff, even over the static the weather wrought.

"Mr. Dodds?"

"Yes?"

"This is Sheriff Baxter."

Jake swallowed and felt a chill thrum through him, even though a distant voice inside him posed the question: *what's left for you to be afraid of?*

"Mr. Dodds?"

"Uh yeah, hi Sheriff. What can I do for you?"

"Is Lenny Quick there with you?"

The chill intensified. "Yes, why?"

"Good," Baxter said, ignoring the question. "Tell him to stay put until I get there."

"All right. But what's—?" The realization that he was talking to nothing but static stopped him and he stared at the receiver for a moment before hanging up.

All sorts of nightmarish scenarios paraded through his mind as he slowly made his way back into the living room, where Lenny was gazing into the fire and humming to himself, but he pushed them away, blaming his own recent loss on the almost overwhelming dread that attempted to drape itself over his shoulders as he took his seat.

"Well?" Lenny asked a few moments later when his expectant look went unnoticed.

"It was uh...it was Sheriff Baxter. The line is buggered with all the snow. I couldn't hear him very well."

"Baxter? What did he want? Is he on to our little speakeasy here?"

Jake tried to think of a lie, or at the very least a semi-truth he could give Lenny to appease him, but the cryptic nature of Baxter's call left no room for anything but the truth.

"It was about you."

The joviality vanished from Lenny's face, replaced with an immediate look of concern that added twenty years to him. "What about me?"

"I don't know. He just asked if you were here. I told him you were and he said to tell you to stay put until he arrives."

"Why?"

"I told you, I don't know. That's all he said and then he hung up. I'm sure it's nothing. Maybe Joanne's car broke down and she's going to be late home or something."

Lenny slowly shook his head. "A sheriff wouldn't come looking for me just to tell me that. He could have told me that over the phone. No, something's happened."

"Aw c'mon, don't go thinking like that," Jake said. "Look out the window, there's nothing but white. Going to be all sorts of traffic problems tonight. I'm sure that's all it is. When you left, was Joanne heading somewhere?"

"Yeah," Lenny said, eyes glassy. "To the store, but that's only a few blocks away. She wouldn't have taken the car."

"She might have, to be out of the cold."

"Jake, I see what you're trying to do, but she didn't drive. Whatever Baxter is coming here to tell me, it isn't about a goddamn breakdown."

Jake couldn't argue further because he knew nothing he'd say would sound believable, even to himself. Lenny was right. When Sheriff Baxter made house calls, it was to ask questions or deliver bad news, and Jake felt certain his own tragedy had attuned him to bad tidings.

And his nerves were singing now.

Mind racing, he almost managed to block out the sound coming from the walls. But then his guard faltered, and his heart skipped a beat, allowing that unmistakable ticking sound an undistracted audience.

Tick-tick-tick.

It ticks for thee.

No, he thought, braced by panic. *Maybe not. Maybe not me at all.*

Lenny rose, tugging Jake from his fearful musings and quieting the deathwatch in the walls.

"What are you doing?"

Lenny's nerves didn't seem to be faring much better. A faint trembling made the glass wobble as he finished his brandy in one gulp and started towards the hall.

"Lenny? What are you doing?" Jake repeated, rising to follow.

"Going home. If something has happened to Joanne, I'm not waiting on a cop to break the news. Might be too late by the time Baxter gets his fat ass through that snow anyway."

"Wait," Jake said and hurried after him into the dark hallway, his knees aflame with pain. In the few seconds it took to reach him, Leroy had already donned his coat and hat and was turning to the door.

"Damn it, wait!" Jake said again, and the near-hysteria in his voice made his friend pause, one hand on the knob.

"Something's happened," Lenny whispered, face grave.

I don't want to be here by myself, Jake almost blurted, immediately shamed by his selfishness. Instead he reached for his coat. "You wanted me to start getting out more," he said, "so if you're not going to wait, I'm coming with you."

He couldn't believe he had said it and only when it was out did he realize how truly small and unfriendly his world had become. In here was loneliness and despair, all measured by the ticking of the deathwatch. Out there was the snow, the loathsome blanket of putrescent mold beneath which Julia slept forever.

Lenny looked about to argue, then sagged and yanked open the front door.

The hostile night roared into their faces as they stepped out into the cold.

* * *

This is insane.

Jake bowed his head against the wet white kisses the sky drove into their faces. Already his skin felt numb and sore, his nose wet and dripping, knees raging with the agony of battling through the ankle-deep drifts that hunkered against the light like protective mothers.

The buildings on both sides of Brennan Street stood like monoliths, fringed with snow and twinkling with the ice that bejeweled them. In some, dim yellow light hugged the frosted windows; in others there was no light at all. Vehicles hunched against the curbs wore scaled skins of white. For such a change in the costume of the earth, noise was expected, but it was as if shredded silence fell from the darkness above.

Lenny was a rail-thin silhouette against the gathering of lights at the head of Brennan Street, his stride purposeful, shoulders tight, hands jammed into his pockets, breath pluming.

Jake squinted, hobbling through the packed snow as fast as he could bear it, praying his knees wouldn't quit on him. The thought of ending up face down in that cold fluffy mold was enough to send shivers rippling through him. "Lenny, slow down," he called, but his cry went either unheard or unheeded.

Lenny moved on, Jake struggling to keep up and wondering, as he guessed his friend was, what the hell Baxter had to report and what he'd do when he found they'd left the house rather than wait.

He prayed Joanne was all right, though a selfish part of him, a mindless, insensitive creature he kept locked away in the foulest recesses of his subconscious, yearned for her to be dead, so Lenny could share in his suffering. So he would no longer have to face the nights alone. Lenny's advice was good, but it welled from a shallow pond in which his friend had never washed, a source that sprung from sympathy, not empathy.

Only through his own loss could he understand Jake's and then, they could help each other through the dark.

Jesus, Jake thought, snapping back to himself, *what the hell is wrong with you?*

He'd been friends with Joanne almost as long as he'd known Lenny. She was a small, stout woman, full of well-meaning bluster but more than capable of adopting an evil temper if it suited her needs. In many ways, she was her husband's opposite and, in this case, at least, the old saying about attraction held true. Their love was as strong as Jake and Julia's had been, even if the Quicks' method of maintaining their relationship was to feign indifference towards each other and to trade sarcastic barbs as much as possible.

That he had wished misfortune upon her, upon them, even momentarily, brought a rush of guilt so strong it was almost debilitating. A quick glance down at the seething white mass engulfing his feet kept him moving.

Six blocks did a respectable impression of twelve before they reached Lenny's house, a small two-story stucco with sagging gutters and a crumbling chimney. A television aerial, lashed to the chimney, stood against the paler patches of wind-wracked sky like a stitch in discolored flesh.

Jake was somewhat surprised to see that Baxter's car was not parked outside. If he had already set out for Jake's house, then they would have met him on the way here. The vehicle he had initially mistaken as the police cruiser as they approached proved to be Joanne's Toyota. From what he could see of it in the grainy light, it appeared undamaged.

Lenny, who had not spoken a word since they'd left Jake's house, suddenly stopped at the foot of the driveway and looked from Jake to the dark house brooding before them as if it was an alien thing, a cold and indifferent replacement for something he had once loved. His face was unreadable.

"Something's going on. I don't like this one bit," he said, just loud enough for Jake to hear. "She always leaves a light on, even when she's out." He shook his head. "*Always.*"

"Maybe she's gone to bed already. Or maybe the bulb blew."

Lenny stared at Jake for a moment before sidestepping a mound of dirty snow presumably left in the wake of a plow, though the street certainly didn't look as if anything but the wind had traveled it in the past few hours.

Heart thudding and unable to shake the feeling that there was something amiss out here, something other than Lenny's deserted house, Jake looked around, his breath emerging as ragged ghosts the wind tore away from him.

Quiet.

Perhaps that was it, he thought. Even for a night like this with apparently no end to the snowfall and the bitter cold, the streets were peculiarly empty. Miriam's Cove was a relatively small town, but the people normally didn't forsake its streets until all hours of the morning. Where were the defiant drivers struggling to get home? Where were the emergency services, the police, the salt trucks? The absence of these mundane, but expected sights, unsettled him. It made him feel as if he and Lenny had missed the imparting of a monumental secret and now, they were left alone in the world with the ghosts of their neighbors circling around them on white waves, waiting for them to realize their folly.

He shuddered and followed Lenny up the driveway where they had to squeeze between the Toyota and a clump of snow that resembled a misshapen hand with weeds sprouting from the knuckles. White eddies spun above their heads like tattered scarves blown from a clothesline. Lenny clumped to the door and when he raised his hand to the doorbell, it was trembling.

"Don't you have the key?" Jake asked.

"I wasn't intending on being out long enough to need one," Lenny said and poked the thin white plastic rectangle until 'Greensleeves' sounded within. It was a jingle Jake hated, but now it seemed horribly ominous because he knew deep inside there was no one in that house to hear it.

"Damn it!"

"Try again," Jake told him, at a loss for a better suggestion.

"She isn't deaf, and she isn't there."

"Then where is she?"

"Would I be standing out here like a fool if I knew?"

"Maybe she's at the police station. Maybe that's what Baxter wanted to tell you."

"Yeah, if he wasn't coming to tell me she's under a white sheet."

Under a white sheet. Jake swallowed. "Don't say that."

"Why? You saying you haven't thought it?"

"This isn't getting us anywhere, Lenny. Maybe we should—"

The street suddenly dimmed, as if something huge had flown overhead. As one, the streetlights winked out.

"What the hell?"

"Power's out," Lenny said and cursed as he launched a kick at the door. Startled, Jake wiped melting snow from his eyelashes and blinked into the dark. The mounds of white gradually began to emerge as if possessed of their own luminescence.

Even in the dark I can see it, Jake thought and shuddered. Though he was wearing a wool-lined overcoat, cold tendrils slithered up his legs and down his neck. He pulled the coat tight around him and lifted one foot, then the other, alternating stances to dissuade the cold and the feeling that the snow was trying to reach his skin.

"What now?" he asked, disturbed by the tremble in his voice.

Lenny was staring at the door, as if still expecting it to fly open.

"Lenny?"

"Maybe you're right," he replied. "Maybe the police station is where she went. We can't stand around in this all night, we'll freeze to death. At least if she isn't there, the cops will know the score. They can drive us back if we need it."

"Right," said Jake and they hurried down the driveway and back onto the street.

They had only gone a few feet, the snow blowing into their faces, when they saw lights up ahead, accompanied by a low growling.

"That a car?" Jake yelled over the wind and he thought he saw Lenny nod.

"Sure looks like it. C'mon."

Jake eventually managed to draw level with Lenny and they trudged on, heads lowered. More than once, Jake had to convince himself that his imagination was on overdrive and that any malevolence he felt at work around him was nothing but a reflection of his own sorrow and the result of weeks of self-imposed isolation. Imagination, nothing more. Had to be. Because rational men did not feel things moving in the snow around their feet.

"Snowplow!" Lenny exclaimed, and Jake looked up, a hand tented over his eyes against the glare of the lights. The growling was louder now and Jake saw that Lenny was right. A truck with a plow blade mounted on the front was slowly making its way toward them.

Jake felt a swell of relief. And then he noticed something odd.

He tugged Lenny's elbow. "Why isn't the blade down?"

"What?"

"The plow blade. It's raised up. There must be almost a foot of snow out here. Why isn't he using the blade?"

Lenny turned back to look at the truck, then shrugged. "Maybe it's damaged. I don't know. Or maybe he's calling it a night."

Jake persisted. "That's Carl Stewart's truck. The guy always has these streets cleared before it gets too deep. For Chrissakes the town gave him an award for it a couple of years back, remember?"

"Yeah."

"So I don't get why he isn't using it now. And look at the way he's driving."

The truck's lights swept across their faces, washing the walls of the house to their right before returning to dazzle them once more.

Lenny moved in the direction of the truck. "You need to calm down a tad," he called over his shoulder. "It's snowing and snowing hard. Ol' Carl's tires are slipping that's all."

But for whatever reason, Jake didn't think so and was about to tell Lenny as much when the truck provided all the confirmation he needed.

The headlights dipped then crawled over the burgeoning plain of snow and fixed on them, turning Lenny into a black scarecrow amid a swarm of snowflakes. The old man tensed, his back hunching into a defensive posture. The truck came on, now less than twenty feet away, its engine roaring, steam billowing from beneath the hood, the upraised blade like a grim smile in the remnants of light it stole from the headlamps.

"Hey!" Lenny called then, waving his arms.

The truck kept coming, the suspension jerking as the vehicle bounced over hard-packed snowdrifts, the tires slipping and sliding.

"Hey, Carl!"

The beams found him again; the engine growled and whined.

Ten feet.

Jake shook his head and reached out a trembling hand to Lenny. "If he's seen us, he'll stop."

Lenny nodded, but continued to wave his arms. In the headlights, Jake noted how very, very old he seemed.

Five feet and now the lights were as bright as the sun in their faces. On instinct, Jake lunged forward and grabbed a handful of Lenny's coat, tugging him hard enough to send them both sprawling on their backs into the snow. The cold was immediate and fierce, and Jake had to struggle not to panic at the feel of it pressing against his skin.

"What did you do *that* for?" Lenny yelled in his face but sat up just in time to find out.

The truck hit a drift hard enough to make the front-end rise, a lower corner of the blade scything through the snow. As Jake and Lenny watched, the truck showed a brief glimpse of its undercarriage before slamming back down, the plow blade twisting until it hung crooked on the grille. The back end of the truck slid out, tugging the truck clear of the drift and sending it slipping backwards toward where the two men had stood watching mere moments before. Snow flew from both sides of the truck as it carved its way past where they sat gasping, spinning one last time on the frozen ground before it met the side of Mabel Brannigan's house and stopped with a bang that sent sparks racing up the wall.

"Jesus," Jake said, easing himself up. Steam from the melted snow and whatever damage had been done to the truck billowed from beneath its crumpled hood. Only one headlight worked now, its single eye blazing into the dark.

Lenny got up and brushed himself off, disbelief contorting his face. He looked about to say something, but instead dropped his gaze and studied the deep grooves the tires had left in the snow not three feet away.

Jake watched him for a moment, then shivered and started toward the truck.

"What are you doing?" Lenny called over the shriek of the wind.

"I want to check on Carl. See if he's okay."

"If he is, let me know. I want to give him what-for. Damn fool almost ran us down."

Jake reached the truck and resisted the urge to warm his hands over the heat flooding from beneath the warped hood. He was so cold now that all consideration for Lenny and his quest had frozen and shattered. He was going home, he decided, which was where he knew he belonged, ghosts of light and shadow bedamned. He would drink the memory of Julia's death and the ticking of that accursed deathwatch away, if only for a few hours, and if it led him to the box beneath the bed again, then so be it. Misery had been his lot for too long now and the ice on his bones only fed it.

Rubbing his hands together, he moved around to the driver side door and tugged on the handle. Something cracked but the door did not open. The glass was pebbled with ice and through it he could see the dim green glow of the instrument panel.

He looked back to where Lenny was still staring at the snow. "Lenny, I need your help. The door's stuck!"

Lenny looked up, but if he replied, his words were stolen by the wind.

"Lenny!"

No answer.

Great.

Jake turned back to the door.

And heard a dull thump as a horribly misshapen head flattened itself against the glass.

"Christ!" Jake jolted, his body immediately flushed with the welcome warmth of adrenaline as his hand clamped over his heart. The heat rapidly abated however, replaced by an inner cold that radiated outward.

The electric control for the window whined and slid down a crack, before stalling, ice grinding and snapping against the rim.

Jake composed himself and moved closer, his heart thumping so hard it almost hurt, his breath wheezing from his lungs.

Too much, he thought. *This is too much to handle. I need to get home.*

It had to be the frosting on the window that made the silhouette in the vehicle seem so out of proportion, for surely no one could survive with that much of their head missing. The green glow from the dashboard illuminated the slope of a bleached white cheek. Shuddering.

"Carl?" Jake called, pressing his hands to the glass and struggling to make out the man's features. "Carl, are you all right in there?"

The shadow bobbed, twitched, moved away from the glass, as if the man was stretching. Or in pain.

"Carl? Can you talk?"

The whisper that floated out from the cracked window made Jake move back a step as he frowned at the window and the flinching figure behind it.

"Yesssssss," it said.

Jake composed himself. He imagined Carl lying in there, bloodied and broken and in urgent need of attention. Now was not the time for fear no matter how unsettling the situation might be.

But God, it was so damn cold.

"Carl, can you move? Are you hurt?"

The figure jerked.

The reply: "They knowwwwww."

"What? I don't understand."

"Theyyyy knowwwwww."

"'They know' what?"

A gurgling sound that might have been a chuckle. Or a man choking on his own blood.

"Carl?"

Silence from inside the truck.

"Carl? Answer me. Can you open the door?"

No answer.

"Carl? Shit!" Jake slapped his palm against the window, knocking away more of the ice. He sighed a cloud of frustration and wiped a hand over his face. His touch was warm against the cold of his cheeks.

Inside the truck, tendrils of shadow rose.

Jake backed away. "Lenny?"

"Is he in one piece?"

Jake was relieved to hear his friend's voice because for just a moment a marrow-freezing panic had taken hold of him, filling him with certainty that when he turned around, Lenny would be gone.

"I don't know," he called back. "Maybe. I can't tell, but I can't get the door open either."

He turned to find Lenny shivering but moving toward him.

"Let's go find help," Jake said. "The door is stuck fast. The longer we spend trying to get him out ourselves, the more chance he stands of dying in there if he's hurt bad enough. Let's just keep going, make our way to the police station and get them to come back for him. It's too goddamn cold here anyway."

He couldn't keep the desperation from his voice and saw it reflected in Lenny's eyes, but no argument was proffered. The night was freezing fast and hard and they both knew they could die out here if the snow got so thick they lost their way.

They could send help. Assuming things didn't get so bad that they ended up being the ones in need of it.

A blast of wind-borne snow lashed into them, making Jake rock on his feet, the icy cold licking against his uncovered neck. "Shit!"

Lenny nodded, teeth clicking together as a shiver rippled through him. "Let's go."

* * *

They continued into the storm, neither of them saying a word.

Jake had never seen the town so quiet, so deserted, and he didn't like it. The absence of the streetlights made an alien landscape of Miriam's Cove, the hollow roar of the sea beyond Patterson's Point lost beneath the faint hissing as the snow fell in endless waves, white dunes heaping themselves high against the somber black buildings. The darkness weighed down upon them, a suffocating thing.

They turned into what memory said was Lewis Avenue, a narrow street which opened out onto Cove Central.

Jake could no longer feel his toes, and the cold was spreading. His coat felt like a sheet of plastic, the thickness of it rendered impotent by his fall in the snow.

When they entered Cove Central, it was as if they'd tripped a wire hidden in the snow. They stopped dead in their tracks, their eyes following the lamps around the thoroughfare as each one stuttered back on, flooding the area with harsh white light.

"That's something at least," Lenny said, with a weary nod. "Maybe now we'll be able to see where we're going."

At the sight of the drifts piling high against the buildings and smothering the cars, Jake felt that knot of fear in his throat tighten. He had thought the snow hungry before, but now that he could fully appreciate the depth and the sheer mass of it, he amended that description. It was not hungry. It was *ravenous*. And no matter how implausible it was to think of snow as anything but innocent, he knew there was something wrong with it. Something terrible *hiding* in it. And like bleeding swimmers in a shark-filled ocean, here the two of them stood, up to their shins in the stuff.

So, let's engage this little madness for a moment, shall we? a quieter, more reasonable voice in his head piped up, *and assume you're right. Why then, has it not already killed you?*

He didn't want to think about that. Couldn't, because aside from the fear and the inexplicable dread he was valiantly attempting to blame on the barbed wire coils of grief, he sensed something bigger at work here, something far more peculiar and unpleasant than unseen things in the snow. He felt *led*. Yes, that was it. He felt as if a hook had snagged in his soul and someone, some*thing* somewhere was slowly reeling him in.

The night had become a strange place, unfamiliar, unkind and filled with latent malice.

Carl Stewart was more than likely freezing to death, if not already dead from his injuries, lying there alone in the battered shell of his snowplow.

Joanne Quick was missing, or worse, a possibility that had to have settled itself on Lenny's shoulders, ageing him terribly as he struggled through the drifts to uncover a truth that might destroy him.

The police station dominated the east end of the square, a narrow two-story red brick building, unremarkable except for the cast iron black bars over the windows, making it look like it had been designed by an aged cowboy pining for the days of the old jails. Clumps of snow sat like sleeping cats in the gutters and atop the windowsills. Over the door, a brass sign marred by verdigris read: MIRIAM'S COVE SHERIFF'S DEPARTMENT.

Lenny paused at the foot of the wide stone steps leading up to the station. He frowned. Jake drew abreast of him and rested his hip against the low wall that bordered the steps, relieving some of the pressure from his aching joints but cementing the cold into his flesh.

Jake didn't have to ask why Lenny had stopped.

Even though the streetlights had come back on, the police station's windows were dark.

They stood together in silence for a moment, then Lenny sighed. "I can't figure it out. Looks like everybody's gone. Are we dreaming?"

Though he knew Lenny wasn't serious, but rather speaking from frustration and more than a little fear, a similar thought had occurred to Jake and, like Lenny, he had been unable to completely dismiss it as fancy. Dreams were not bound by natural law and wasn't that how things seemed in the town tonight? Jake wished it to be so, some inner part of him warmed by the idea of waking in his bed to find that none of this had happened outside of his own feverish imaginings.

But the hope was weak.

The cold was real, too real to pin on a dream.

*And let's face it buddy, even if it was a dream, the real world ain't so friggin'
hot for you these days, is it?*

"Maybe we should head back just in case Baxter's waiting at your
house."

"Maybe," Jake said. "But I'm a little leery about following your
suggestions after that last one about me getting out of the house." He
grinned feebly and folded his arms. "Let's check out the station first.
Maybe they'll at least have some still-warm coffee. If we can get in at all."

Lenny nodded and headed up the steps. Jake followed, wincing. He
whispered a silent prayer that the door would be unlocked.

Just one break. Please. Just one.

Lenny slipped his fingers around the brass door handle, thumbed
down the button and pulled. Ice crunched and tumbled from the crack in
the jamb, but the door did not move.

Jake sagged. "It's a goddamn night for locked doors, isn't it?"

Lenny didn't reply, but turned, a scowl on his face.

"Can you see inside?"

"What difference does it make?"

"Maybe they just locked the place up because of the storm?"

Lenny offered him a tired smile. "For a grieving man, you're sure
quick with the sunshine."

"Call it desperation. I'm sick to death of this cold."

"Then maybe we should kick the doors down."

"Right, breaking and entering into a police station. That'll be one for
the books. Assuming of course we had the strength in our legs to even try
without crippling ourselves."

Lenny snorted and gestured out over the thoroughfare. "Doesn't look
like there'd be many witnesses though, huh?"

"No. Guess not."

With a satisfied nod, Lenny turned back to the door. "Oh JESUS!"

Jake's scalp prickled, and he took two paces back from the door,
almost expecting it to explode outward with the same force that now held
his heart in its hands. "What? What is it?"

Lenny was standing stock-still, arms by his sides, staring in through
the rectangular glass panel on the left side of the door.

"Lenny?"

"I...I saw someone."

"Saw who?" Ignoring the fresh bursts of pain that crisscrossed his knees at the suddenness of his movements and propelled by renewed hope, Jake rushed to join Lenny at the window. He almost screamed when he saw a white, hollow-eyed face leering back at him from the glass, but then it shrank and vanished only to reappear at the behest of Lenny's breath. Condensation, nothing more, but it had almost been enough to prompt those invisible hands into giving his heart a final squeeze. With a sigh, he squinted to see through the window.

Beyond the glass, the suffused light from the street allowed him a glimpse of a pale rectangular smudge which might have been the desk sergeant's computer. Like imitation moonlight, the silvery glow shining through the high windows sent fractured streaks across the tile-floor hallway. The hall ran toward the back of the building until darkness claimed it.

The station seemed as deserted as the rest of town, but in there, as out here, there were plenty of hiding places.

Lenny's tremulous breath rumbled in his ear.

Still scanning the hall, Jake asked: "What did you see?"

"A woman."

"Did you recognize her?"

"No."

"Well...why didn't you try and get her attention?"

He felt Lenny shrug. "The way she looked, I didn't *want* to get her attention."

"How did she look?"

"Dead," Lenny said simply. "Or damn close."

Lenny didn't answer, but his breathing had slowed. Jake guessed whatever had spooked him had already registered itself as silly now that he'd said it aloud. But that still left the question of who was inside the station. Jake cupped his hands around his face and tried one last time to see if he could detect movement from inside.

Lenny's breathing quickened almost immediately, thundering in Jake's ear and heating the flesh there.

Inside the station, nothing moved.

"In all my years in this town I don't think I've ever seen the police station locked up, for any reason. So why now?"

No answer.

"It's bad but not bad enough to evacuate a building as solid as this one, don't you think?"

No answer.

We have to get home, or we'll die out here, Jake thought as a wave of cold rushed up his back, making his teeth chatter.

"We better go back," he said.

Lenny's only response was his frightened breathing, now so loud that after a few moments Jake pushed away and rubbed a tickle from his ear. "Would y—?" he began but stopped just as fast, one hand still clamped to the side of his head.

He noticed two things at once.

First, it was no longer snowing, but any joy he might have felt at that realization drained from him almost immediately.

Because Lenny was gone.

But he was just here! Right next to me. Breathing like a horse in my bloody ear!

His own breath shriveled before his face then, eyes widening as something dreadful occurred to him.

You only thought *it was Lenny.*

With a furtive glance around the town square from his vantage point atop the steps, Jake yelled Lenny's name, once, twice, then waited.

The town listened but did not respond.

And after some inestimable time spent quivering and weeping uncontrollably, Jake did something he hadn't done in twelve years, something his aching legs protested at every turn.

He ran.

* * *

Someone was whispering to him, but he would not listen.

Instead he ran on, lurching forward in unsteady strides like a wounded deer, clutching his coat to his chest even though it was not open, as if doing so would keep his heart in his chest long enough for him to make it home.

Home. A million miles away now in this hostile frozen wasteland in which normality seemed to be frozen too. Everywhere lay indistinct figures, smooth and glittering beneath their cold blankets, sometimes moving in the periphery of his vision, sometimes shuddering like yawning dogs, sometimes whispering to him in a language he did not understand, nor want to.

The cold rattled him as he lurched along, the snow accepting his booted feet, hampering his progress as he sank with each frantic step. The tears froze on his face, his lower lip quivering as he sobbed.

Home. All the demons he feared beyond the walls of his home, all the night things that whispered to him of his cowardice, all the sounds that made him feel crowded and yet hopelessly alone, that detestable ticking like tiny bones being tapped together, all of it he would suffer gladly now. Nothing could possibly be worse than this. Nothing, for it was not the snow and the things beneath it he feared any more, but what they represented. Madness, pure and simple. Somewhere along the line—maybe when Julia died—his mind had split, crumbled, and betrayed him, sketching nightmares for him to suffer in his waking hours. Waiting until he was most vulnerable. Waiting until he was alone and cold and terrified. It was the simplest explanation and the most horrible one.

And yet, the possibility offered hope.

For madness, there might be a cure.

For a reality turned nightmare, none.

He emerged from his own panicked thoughts to find he had reached Mabel Brannigan's house. Carl Stewart's truck was still there but Carl was not. A fresh skin of snow hugged the metal. The door of the pickup swung in the wind, the green glow from the dashboard oozing onto the empty seats. Beneath the door was a ragged hole, ringed with some kind of dark matter, and from the hole a two-foot-high mound of snow crossed the street in a zigzagging pattern.

Something had tunneled here.

The deposited snow ran like a barrier across the road, but Jake crossed it in a hurry, and without incident, though the hair on his neck stood on end as he drew one leg and then the other across it and hurried on, his breath warm around his face. Every inhalation felt as though he was drawing in sand and when he coughed, he thought his lungs would explode.

Then Lenny's house loomed, just as before.

With one difference.

The front door was open, granting him a view of nothing but absolute darkness within.

He considered venturing inside—at least he'd be out of the cold—but with all that had happened, he decided it was best to get home, to get safe. Then maybe, he'd come back, or call someone to...

Forget it. Keep moving. And he did, feeling as if someone had strapped still-burning coals around his knees.

There would be nothing to find in Lenny's house. At least, nothing he wished to find. Something was happening, whether instigated by his own bruised mind or not, he couldn't tell. People were vanishing, the town had changed, and malevolent things lurked beneath the snow. Some tangle in his synapses had made Miriam's Cove a ghost town.

Alone, he hurried on, ignoring the faintest suggestion of frenzied pale tendrils emerging from that oblong of dark that was Lenny's front door. If they were really there, then so be it, but nothing short of a broken neck would make him look in that direction. Not now, not when he was so close to home.

Fighting the white road, the all-consuming mold, the blanket beneath which the dead lay dreaming, a line from a poem he had read in his younger, healthier, saner days came whispering through the dark inside his head: "'Fall, winter, fall; for he/Prompt hand and headpiece clever/Has woven a winter robe/And made of earth and sea/His overcoat for ever.'" A.E. Housman, he recalled, mildly amused to find he had recited the stanza aloud. A poem he had read for students in his high school teaching days, days long gone, along with everything else, along with the history teacher he had met and fallen in love with there. Housman had known the deal, Jake knew, securing his suspicions of winter's wrath in the lines of a poem to escape ridicule and accusations of madness, accusations Jake couldn't hope to escape now that the projections of it had turned the whole world around him into a hollow white nightmare.

Keep going!

He did, hobbling, grimacing, hissing air through teeth cold as headstones, squinting through eyes that saw as if through a film of ice.

And then, his street, silent as a tomb, buried in snow. His house, smoke ghost tearing itself from the chimney, light in the window. He stopped, fresh tears dripping down his cheeks, scarcely daring to believe it could be true. Light in the window. Warm amber light.

And in the driveway, Sheriff Baxter's police cruiser, gleaming. No sirens, no wailing. Quiet. Doors closed. No damage.

Jake nodded and cracked a smile from which inner heat seemed to flow. This was right. This was the way it was supposed to be. He knew what he would find in there. Warmth, safety, sanity, and Sheriff Baxter warming his hands by the fire, angry that Lenny and Jake hadn't waited for him. Joanne would be fine.

She tripped and hurt her ankle on the ice, Baxter would tell him. *Nothing critical. I sent Deputy Harlow to take her to the hospital. She's fine. Be out by morning. Now where the hell is her damn fool husband gone? Probably figured out that's where she'd be and walked over there.* Here Baxter would shake his head. *Bad idea for a man his age in this weather, let me tell you.*

And Jake would smile, agree and offer the Sheriff a glass of something strong and the lawman would take it, because even lawmen were not impervious to this kind of cold. Then they would sit and wait in the warmth for word from Lenny.

Grinning now, Jake took a step toward his house.

And the lights went out.

No. Oh please...no!

In the snow around him something moved. No, not something. The snow *itself* was moving, slowly undulating like a sheet in the wind. Whispers, struggling to imitate the breeze but failing to sound even remotely natural, swept up from the rolling white, overlapping into a nonsensical chorus it hurt the mind to hear. Jake, despite his panic, remembered when he had heard it before, close to his ear and hidden in what he had mistakenly thought was Lenny's breathing.

Full insanity. Had to be. Such things simply did not, could not happen. There were laws that dictated it. And yet, all around him the snow erupted, tunnels tearing toward him, slick white tendrils bursting from the drifts and waving at him, opaque eyes unblinking in the darkness. The ground shuddered, and his feet sank further, though this time it was not the snow that hugged his ankles. It was fingers, malleable slivers of ice that slid around the exposed skin there and held tight.

His bladder let go but he was only dimly aware of it, less aware when the urine froze halfway down.

The clouds of his breath caressed the facial features of things which had preferred to remain invisible as they circled him, but he could see them now. Grinning, their white eyes alight with fierce intelligence, with awareness...

They know, Carl Stewart had said, and it was clear now that they did. They knew everything. They knew he had tried to take his life in a drunken fit of suicidal hysteria. They knew the barrel had been in his mouth even after he'd called Lenny. They knew he had pulled the trigger and the gun had jammed.

But most of all, they knew about the cancer that had eaten his wife and the pillow that had stopped her breathing.

The churned-up snow stopped mere inches from his feet as the tunnel digger ceased its labors.

They know...

Trembling turned to convulsing as if these things, whatever they were, had stripped him naked. The cold fed on him and he shrieked at it, at them, at everything that had brought him on this path, to this moment, to his certain death.

"Go away!" he screamed at them, his mind unable to cope with the sheer amount of movement that registered in his vision. Here, a hand only slightly smaller than Carl Stewart's truck, scarred and patterned with intricate loops and swirls, clutching at the sky with fish belly fingers, its wrist blue where it emerged from the snow. There, a dark figure, flinching as if beaten by unseen fists, its eyes elliptical slits stuffed with shards of glowing ice. To his left, a woman danced like a marionette with too few strings, her hair fashioned from the snow itself, clumps of it obscuring her face. She was naked, her body blue, breasts full, nipples black, legs studded with icicles that gleamed as she swung in the arms of an invisible partner. To his right, a glass scarecrow hissed and bowed in supplication. But not to Jake.

Whimpering, he watched as a hole formed at his feet, the snow pulled down by several pale hands scrabbling frantically.

"Please..."

But even as the words staggered over his trembling lips, he knew they would go unheard. They already knew all they needed to.

The hole widened. The hands vanished into the dark and then slowly, slowly, something started to emerge.

Jake pulled, desperately trying to tear himself free of the snow, but it was no use, the spikes of pain in his arthritic knees only served to remind him how old, how weak, how cold and how foolish he was. And how pointless it was to try and escape.

A face rose smiling from the hole, a gaunt weathered face with eyes like cold suns. The shock of recognition almost knocked Jake backward, a move that might have left him with two shattered ankles so tight was the grip of the snow.

"We know," said Lenny, or the shell of what had once been his best friend. Jake fell to his knees and felt the resistance from the clutching snow, allowing him the fall but not his freedom.

Lenny still wore his coat, hands in pockets, hat askew on his head. If not for the eyes, the impression would have been flawless.

Jake lifted his head to look into the creature's face. "Why you?" he asked. "Why did they hurt you, Lenny?"

The Lenny-thing tilted its head. "We know. And you must know too."

Jake looked longingly towards his house. It was dark now, and unwelcoming, and he could hear the faintest of ticking sounds echoing from inside. The memory of Lenny's voice, spoken from fireside safety, spoken on the fringes of a nightmare, joined the deathwatch echo.

"You mentioned dying. I was wondering if you remembered the last time we talked about it. What you told me..."

And now he did remember, more than he'd remembered before, as the cold shattered the walls of his resistance.

He had called Lenny that night, had wept his sorrows into the phone. But that was not all. Amid the pleas and the desperation, there had also been a confession.

"Jake, calm down. I can't understand you."

"—her!"

"Talk into the phone. I can't—"

"I killed her, Lenny. I fucking killed her because I couldn't watch her dying in front of me and now, I want to be with her. Help me!"

"Oh my God..."

Lenny knew. But because he was a loyal friend, he had chosen to keep it a secret and that secret had killed him because these things, these creatures of guilt and punishment, had known too.

The thing in Lenny's clothes grinned, exposing a mouthful of icicle teeth.

Tick, tick, tick, the watch wound down, the same watch Julia had worn in her deathbed as she struggled feebly against the pillow, her hands trapped beside her face. The same watch he had used to count the seconds until her death, to count the beats of her heart.

Both had stopped running at the same time.

He swallowed and hugged himself. *This is how they mean to kill me,* he thought. *They'll keep me here, in the cold, until it stops my heart.*

Silence.

Someone standing behind him reached a slim pale blue hand over his shoulder, grazing his cheek with its rough skin and clamping down hard enough to register pain over the numbing cold.

He turned, shivering, teeth chattering so violently they must surely break. And his breath caught in his throat.

The woman standing there wore an ill-fitting expression of love that faded and changed to cold blue rage while he watched, stricken, paralyzed by utter, unbridled horror.

The hush deepened.

"I'm...s-s-sorry. I swear I am," he sobbed and sensed, rather than felt, them all descend upon him as one hissing mass.

It began to snow.

recommended books

I read both *The Shining* and *The Terror* during massive snowstorms, and I've never forgotten how thrilling and immersive those experiences were. So, if you find yourself snuggled up in your favorite chair by the window, cocoa in hand, looking for something to read while feathery flakes of snow whisper down into the cold white world outside, here are some recommendations to chill the blood...

The Shuddering by Ania Ahlborn
The Brief History of the Dead by Kevin Brockmeier
The Well by Jack Cady
Midnight Sun by Ramsey Campbell
Who Goes There? by John W. Campbell
Dark Hollow by John Connolly
The Boy Who Drew Monsters by Keith Donohue
Wolf Winter by Cecilia Ekbäck
Hold the Dark by William Giraldi
Ararat by Christopher Golden
Snowblind by Christopher Golden
Generation Loss by Elizabeth Hand
NOS4A2 by Joe Hill
The Woman in Black by Susan Hill
The Snowman's Children by Glen Hirshberg
The Turn of the Screw by Henry James
The Silent Land by Graham Joyce
The Hunger by Alma Katsu
Dreamcatcher by Stephen King
Misery by Stephen King
The Shining by Stephen King

Icebound by Dean Koontz
Face by Tim Lebbon
White by Tim Lebbon
Let the Right One In by John Ajvide Lindqvist
At the Mountains of Madness by H.P. Lovecraft
Bone White by Ronald Malfi
Snow by Ronald Malfi
Stranded by Bracken MacLeod
Snowblind by Michael McBride
The Winter People by Jennifer McMahon
The Stupidest Angel by Christopher Moore
The Winter Ghosts by Kate Mosse
Waiting Out Winter by Kelli Owen
White is for Witching by Helen Oyeyemi
Dark Matter by Michelle Paver
Thin Air by Michelle Paver
I'm Thinking of Ending Things by Iain Reid
The Wolves of Midwinter by Anne Rice
Midwinter of the Spirit by Phil Rickman
Dead White by Alan Ryan
Chasing the Dead by Joe Schreiber
Frankenstein by Mary Shelley
A Winter Haunting by Dan Simmons
The Abominable by Dan Simmons
The Terror by Dan Simmons
A Simple Plan by Scott Smith
The Blizzard by Vladimir Sorokin
Ghost Story by Peter Straub

about the author

Born and raised in a small harbor town in the south of Ireland, Kealan Patrick Burke knew from a very early age that he was going to be a horror writer. The combination of an ancient locale, a horror-loving mother, and a family full of storytellers, made it inevitable that he would end up telling stories for a living. Since those formative years, he has written five novels, over a hundred short stories, six collections, and edited four acclaimed anthologies. In 2004, he was honored with the Bram Stoker Award for his novella *The Turtle Boy*.

Kealan has worked as a waiter, a drama teacher, a mapmaker, a security guard, an assembly-line worker at Apple Computers, a salesman (for a day), a bartender, landscape gardener, vocalist in a grunge band, curriculum content editor, fiction editor at Gothic.net, and, most recently, a fraud investigator.

When not writing, Kealan designs book covers through his company Elderlemon Design.

Several of his books have been optioned for film.

Visit him on the web at www.kealanpatrickburke.com or on Twitter @kealanburke

Made in the USA
Columbia, SC
20 October 2023

24741148R00059